## *The switch of bags was not an accident.*

Since I was one of only a handful of people who would recognize what the bag contained, I was convinced this was true.

The suitcase was an exact replica, which isn't so weird—how many black, wheeled carry-on models are there, after all?

Where could it have gotten mixed-up? At security, the van, the security checkpoint? But I hadn't paid attention. I'd been running late.

Inside I found a white box. Jewelry, I thought, opening it—after all, jewels were my stock in trade. Judging by the rest of the suitcase's contents, the jewelry would be something understated. Probably gold, expensive.

It was expensive, all right.

Pillowed in the cotton batting was a jewel. A diamond. Katerina's Blood.

Not only was it huge, it was very rare and storied, this jewel.

It was even cursed.

Dear Reader,

A couple of years ago, I had a chance to tour Scotland. It wasn't one of those places I'd ached to visit my whole life long, but the chance arrived and I leapt upon it—I'm a travel bug and love to go almost anywhere.

And wouldn't you know it? I fell madly in love—with the landscape, the culture, the people. I hardly knew at the time that Sylvie Montague was going to arrive in my life with her red leather miniskirts and talent for finding trouble, but arrive she did, driving a hot Alfa Romeo along twisting roads through tiny villages, with a skill only her Formula One father could have taught her.

Along with Sylvie came her unrequited love, and a devastatingly sexy European who may or may not be a bad guy. Sylvie's stuck with him, anyway, and how she gets herself out of trouble was a blast to write. I hope you'll enjoy it, too.

I love to hear from readers. Write to me via e-mail at ruthwind@gmail.com. Or visit my Web site at www.barbarasamuel.com.

May the wind be ever at your back!

Ruth

# Ruth Wind

# The Diamond Secret

Silhouette®

# BOMBSHELL™

Published by Silhouette Books

**America's Publisher of Contemporary Romance**

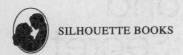

**SILHOUETTE BOOKS**

ISBN 0-373-51397-6

THE DIAMOND SECRET

www.SilhouetteBombshell.com

**Printed in U.S.A.**

# RUTH WIND

is the award-winning author of both contemporary and historical romance novels. She lives in the mountains of the Southwest with her two growing sons and many animals in a hundred-year-old house the town blacksmith built. The only hobby she has since she started writing is tending the ancient garden of irises, lilies and lavender beyond her office window, and she says she can think of no more satisfying way to spend a life than growing children, books and flowers. Ruth Wind also writes women's fiction under the name Barbara Samuel. You can visit her Web site at www.barbarasamuel.com.

Thanks to Alan McPhaetor for the good company
and good information

# *Prologue*

Few objects on earth can inflame the lusts of man as certain jewels will. They contain the one beauty that never fades or dies or changes— they embody power, sex, money. A single jewel, small enough to cradle in the palm of your hand, can be equal to the worth of a third world nation. They're eternal, undying, mysterious, storied.

And nothing can bring out the evils of man like the lust to possess a particular jewel....

—Sylvie Montague, addressing Estate
Jewelers International

*Ayr, Scotland*

There's always a man, isn't there, when things are about to hit the fan? In my case, there were three. One I'd loved a very long time. One had betrayed me. And one swept me into a drama I only half wished to escape.

The adventure began when I opened my suitcase in a hotel on the west coast of Scotland and learned that that somewhere over the Atlantic, someone had switched bags with me. Instead of two dozen pairs of (expensive!) thongs and a pair of red leather pants, I found a diamond.

A very *large* diamond.

Large and legendary, so infamous that I could not, for a long space of breaths, do anything but stare at the spectacular beauty of it, tucked in cotton batting by some unknown person.

I picked it up knowing two things. One: it was no accident that I, jewel expert Sylvie Montague, should be holding in her hand 80-something karats of medieval diamond.

Two: it was undoubtedly stolen.

Standing in a hotel room that smelled of the sea, I held the jewel in my hand, breathless, and tried to think when the bags could have been switched. I'd carried mine on the plane from San Francisco and shoved it into the very last remaining space in the overhead compartment. I couldn't think of anyone opening the bin before the end of the flight, when I'd opened it myself and pulled my suitcase out.

But somewhere, someone had switched it. In my grasp was a diamond I had certainly not packed. My hands shook as I held it up to the light. My heart pounded.

It was unmistakable.

Katerina's Blood.

Oh my God.

# Chapter 1

In the treatise on gems by Buddhabhatta (Finot, "Les Lapidaires Indiens," Paris, 1896) we read: A diamond, a part of which is the color of blood or spotted with red, would quickly bring death to the wearer, even if he were the Master of Death.

—*Folklore of Diamonds*

*Three hours earlier*

The flight from San Francisco to Glasgow was a miserable one. Not that there's any such thing as a *good* transcontinental flight. They're always too long, too boring, too cramped and not even the luxury of my own back-of-the-seat movies does much to alleviate the agony of sitting still for that long.

The only decent thing about the whole flight was a guy across the aisle. Dark hair, cut close to his head, a little shadow of beard, a sharply cut mouth with full lips. I pegged him as Continental, and then spent some of the long, boring time trying to figure out why. The sweater, perhaps—a wool turtleneck. His clean, long hands. The shape of his mouth, which looked like it might shape words with long, rolling *r*'s. French, maybe.

At the end of a flight like that, all you want is to get off the freaking plane. It felt good to just walk down the concourse pulling my bag, stretching out the cramped muscles, shaking off the thickness of over-breathed air. I had checked no luggage, so made straight for the car rental counter, mentally crossing my fingers that my father had come through for me.

When I said my name, "Sylvie Montague," the buzz-cut, redheaded youth behind the counter blinked.

"Aye," he said, his eyes widening. "It's all set up. I've got it right here." With a gesture of reverence, he handed me the keys to an Alpha Romeo Spider.

Great car. Fast, elegant, very European. My father *had* come through for me. I grinned and slapped the keys in my pocket. "Thanks."

"Are you related to him?" the youth asked. "To Gordon Montague, I mean."

"Mmm. My father."

"He's the greatest racer ever."

"Thanks. I'll tell him." When I turned around, I nearly slammed into a burly man right behind me. With a balding head of gingery hair and pale freckles across his forehead and nose, his ruddy cheeks made him look as if he were about to have a heart attack on the spot. I forgave him the glare he leveled on me.

"Sorry," I said.

He grumbled something and shoved by me.

The car was in the parking lot, taut and silver, worthy of the admiring stroke I gave her sleek rear. I opened the driver door and was stripping off my coat when the beautiful—Frenchman?—from the plane walked by.

"Is she yours?" he asked, cocking a brow toward the car.

The accent was not French. It sounded eastern European, not quite Russian, not quite Polish. I couldn't place it, but it was charming anyway.

I grinned. "For today."

"Sometimes, that's all we need, no?"

"Yes." I nodded and made a show of unlocking the trunk. He walked down the length of her, admiring the curves swooping over the tires, the line of the hood. One hand was loosely tucked in the pocket of his corduroy slacks, and a leather jacket hung in the crook of his elbow. Every inch of him declared a casual Continentalness, that whiff of minor royalty. I liked his very thick, dark, glossy hair, a touch too long, extravagant with ringlets, and his beautiful white hands, long-fingered, artistic-looking.

I tucked my suitcase and coat into the trunk. Or boot, I suppose, since I was now in the UK again. I asked, "Is this your first trip to Scotland?"

"No. I have many friends here. You?"

"I'm here on business, and visiting family."

"Ah." He glanced toward the street, appeared to be thinking something over.

When he didn't speak, I slammed the boot closed and smiled. "Enjoy your trip."

His eyes were a strong blue when he looked back at me. "Are you in a hurry? Would you like to have a little supper with me?"

I had to shake my head. "Sorry. I have to be somewhere in an hour."

"Ah," he said, and cocked an eyebrow, obviously assuming I was going to meet my lover. I didn't dissuade him, only smiled slightly. His shrug said there was never any harm in trying. "Perhaps we'll meet again another day."

I lifted a shoulder.

Several other passengers were picking out their cars from the lot, and I saw the red-faced pit bull from the rental car line. He climbed into a Nissan and slammed the door. He made me think of a cartoon, squished into the little car, and if his expression was anything to go by, he was Not Pleased.

A sudden thought made me wonder if he was paparazzi. They only bugged me now and then, but with my father racing this week and my own visibility on the jewel case—which they were calling the King Pin's Crown Jewels—I'd probably have to put up with them.

"Au revoir," said the Continental.

I'd been distracted by the other man. "Au revoir," I said and fit my key into the door lock. He slung a slim leather bag over his shoulder and headed for a different section of cars.

*Too bad,* I thought. I have no illusions about the permanence of holiday love affairs—or, well, love affairs in general—but there was no harm in a little flirtation. He looked as if he'd be one of those very dramatic and passionate sorts, the kind who likes to tuck a woman into his arm and kiss her wildly. It gets old to be smothered like that after a while, but it's nice for the short term. And really, it had been a while.

I glanced over my shoulder to see if the red-cheeked man had gone, and he was pulling into traffic. Not a danger, then. I dashed after the Continental.

"Um…" We hadn't exchanged names. "Wait!"

He paused. I held up a finger and tugged my card out of my wallet, scribbled a number on the back and gave it to him. "I'll be in Ayr for a few days, if you're in the neighborhood."

"But *I* am going to Ayr!" he exclaimed in surprise.

"You are?" I echoed. It's not a particularly large town, a holiday hamlet favored by Glaswegians in the summertime. But it was not yet quite April, and the weather was too cold and unstable for seaside retreats. "I didn't think anyone visited Ayr until June."

He inclined his head slightly. "Perhaps not. I have a good friend there." He looked at the card, raised dark eyes to mine. "Sylvie. That's French, no?"

"My grandmother's name." A Parisian swept off her feet by a Scottish soldier in WWII. "She lives in Ayr. That's who I'm going to see this afternoon." I looked at my watch and realized I needed to get moving. Backing away, a palm over the face of the watch as if to hide the time from myself, I said, "I need to be there by tea."

"Will you be free later, then?" His smile showed slightly uneven, but very white teeth. "Shall we have supper?"

I thought about the requirements of the evening. No doubt a cousin or two would be at my grandmother's house, and there would be catching up to do. Then I could plead exhaustion—it wouldn't be far from the truth—and get to the hotel by seven. "At the Drover pub, at eight?"

He tucked my card into his front pocket. His blue eyes glittered. "I will look forward to it."

I realized as I got in the car that I still had not asked his name.

It seemed a portent, somehow.

## Chapter 2

The 4 C's of diamond grading are Cut, Color, Clarity and Carat Weight, but remember there is a full 13-point grading scale, and the best consumer will understand each point.

—www.costellos.com.au

I headed for Ayr on the A-77, just ahead of the worst of rush hour. It's called the killer road for a reason. Narrow, unpredictable, given to odd lane shifts and sudden roundabouts—exactly the reason I love it. I learned to drive at my father's knee, one of the only things he has ever been good for. Like him, I love fast, sharp and quick. Rush hour is just too congested to be much fun.

Probably just as well I had to limit my speed. My reflexes were probably not their best after such a long flight. Rolling down the windows to let the cool wind blow the jet lag out of my brain, I turned the radio to a Glasgow station pouring out a Scottish version of heavy metal. The voices between songs were so thickly accented I could only understand about every third word, but it didn't matter.

Home.

After a fashion. My mother's home, anyway, a place I spent a lot of time as a girl, splitting time between my father and mother. I was there to work at the request of the Glasgow police department, to evaluate and catalogue a cache of jewels recently seized when a high-profile drug runner known as The Swede was murdered two weeks ago.

The jewels stunned everyone, and various theories were batted around before they decided to call me. The investigator in charge had followed a case last summer when the Egyptian police called me in to help recover the Nile Sapphire, a very old and fabled jewel. The inspector also read that my mother was Scottish and trusted me a little more because of it. He called to see if I'd consult, had offered airfare and a hotel room in Glasgow for the duration.

It was a no-brainer. I was coming up on the one-year anniversary of my divorce, and didn't want to spend the week moping back at home in San Francisco. It had also been a while since I'd seen my mother's family, and although I do travel a bit for the job, most of it is pretty dull stuff—assessing estates and that sort of thing. Mostly, of course, I'm crouched over dusty brooches in mildewy rooms, giving myself a crick in the neck as I peer through a loupe and take notes on clarity and color.

Another reason driving was so thrilling. There was nothing like getting on a tight, challenging road in a good machine after a long day of estate assessment.

Or a nine-hour flight.

I turned up the radio, tucked a flying lock of hair behind my ear and passed a vivid blue Fiat driven by a man in shirtsleeves and dark sunglasses. I saw him take note of my blond hair and sexy blouse, and, with a slight grin, I gunned it.

It would be a pleasure to comb through the jewels of a drug lord, who'd had, by all accounts, very good taste. The inspector had mentioned several sapphires in particular; thought they might be connected to a group that had gone missing more than six years ago. I was excited to take a look at them.

The blue Fiat zoomed by me, and I glanced over curiously. The man driving was not thrilled to have been passed up by a girl. I saw it the minute he glanced over at me, a little rumbling of competition. A growl of his engine.

I smiled. The Spider was a dream car, more than enough for an itty-bitty challenge like this. The traffic was heavy and I wouldn't be an idiot and risk other people's lives, but I'd play for a minute with Tom Fiat.

Pressing down with my foot on the accelerator, I coaxed the Spider next to the Fiat, and edged ahead, just enough to let him know I was doing it on purpose. He gunned it, and tugged ahead, but the Spider wasn't even panting yet, and I caught him easily, rumbling along beside him.

We sailed around a tight curve, bound on either side by rolling fields, coming up behind a semi that was lumbering along on the right.

Signs warned that the road would narrow to two lanes in 1000 meters, 500.

I knew I could take him. Through my body, I could feel the smooth connection between the machine and myself, as if the engine were part of my fingers, my arms. I rode the curve, hugging the road, and passed the truck. Wind whipped my hair around my neck. I downshifted, whirled around the turn. On the right, cars going the opposite direction roared by, mere inches away across the dividing line.

I grinned to myself. Exhilarating!

Tom Fiat had steam coming out of his ears as he whizzed around the lorry to catch up with me.

Everyone in Scotland drives as if they're muttering "bastard" under their breath, anyway, and there's a reckless fatalism that can give even me a few moments of pause.

Still. It was a point of pride just now. I held to the lead.

Ahead loomed the narrowing lanes. Tom was about to kill someone. I let up on the gas, hugged the road to the left to let him pass and waved as he went by. His face was a dull red of fury, and I laughed to myself. No one ever expects a woman to drive the way I do.

But most women don't learn to drive from a world-class Formula One driver. My father, the legendary American Gordon Montague, is one of the most revered drivers on the planet at the moment, and I've no doubt the legend will live long after he kills himself in some spectacular wreck at Monaco or Barcelona. He'd like that, dying dramatically in some glamorous spot, mourned publicly by whatever young wife he happened to have picked up at the moment.

Dear old dad.

I was glad of the car, and wished, briefly, that he was with me. It's been a while since we'd had any time together. I was tempted to ask him to meet me in Glasgow after the Malaysian Grand Prix in Kuala Lampur, but I had a feeling he'd say no. Scotland makes him feel guilty.

As well it should.

Scotland is my mother's place, and I admired it now through her eyes—a countryside as calming as the wind blowing in my window. It was lambing season, and little balls frolicked in the fields among the more sedate sheep and the odd shaggy red cow. Trees bent halfway sideways belied the bucolic scene, showing what the winds are like around here, but on this bright day, I could even see the island of Arran in the distance, an uneven line of pale blue mountains on the horizon.

I'd opted to stay in a hotel rather than with a relative, even though there are several I could choose from in my mother's hometown. Which is actually the trouble. If I picked one, I'd hurt someone else's feelings. A hotel room is easier.

The job in Glasgow would start in a couple of days. My plan was to knock around Ayr and the seaside of my childhood, visit my aunts and cousins, make a stop to put flowers on my mother's grave, then head back to Glasgow for the assessment, maybe catch some shows or something.

Since I didn't know that giant diamond was stashed away in my bag, I stopped first at my grandmother's house. She lived on a well-kept street of what we'd call fourplexes. Row houses, they call them, and there are thousands and thousands of them all throughout the U.K., built right after the war.

That would be *the* war, World War II.

My grandmother lived on the end of her building. Her windows were polished, as were all the windows on the street, and red tulips had pushed their way up into the spring air. She'd no doubt been waiting for me—sitting with her next-door neighbor, Anna, and a blue budgie who sang to her from his perch—because she flung open the door. *"Ma cher!"* the elder Sylvie cried. "I am so happy to see you!"

I dashed up the narrow sidewalk to hug her. Tiny as a sparrow, her white hair now cut neatly around her sharply angled face, she was still a beauty at seventy-eight. She had nary a wrinkle. "Come in, *ma poulette!*" she cried. "Have you had your tea?"

"No, of course not! Not if I had a chance to have your coffee and some cake."

Over my shoulder, my grandmother glared. I turned to see a battered Mini crawling down the street. "Go on with you!" she cried, sounding more Scottish than French. "Nosy rats. They've been nosing around all day."

Papparazzi again. I was tempted to flip them off, but it would only give them what they were after—something to print in their trashy little journals. My hugging an old woman wouldn't do much for their circulation.

In the vestibule, she took my coat and led me into the tiny sitting room, where her best friend Anna waited. Slim and thoughtful, Anna had always been one of my favorites. She told wonderful stories of her girlhood and the Scotland that existed before the war, and she did not suffer fools lightly.

"Hello, Sylvie," she said. "We've just seen your father on television."

"Really." I settled in the place they made for me before the fire, feeling as pampered as a beloved princess. "Tell me all about it."

In the street outside the window, the beat-up Mini rolled by again. Something about the man behind the wheel was seedier or grimmer or something than the average—even average tabloid—photographer. I narrowed my eyes and stood up to watch him go by. He was very interested in my car.

"What is it, dear?" Grandmother asked.

I shook my head, unwilling to worry them. "Just that photographer again."

But I wondered.

# Chapter 3

KATERINA'S BLOOD, diamond with ruby inclusion; 83 karats; first recorded ownership: 1253, Romania. Supposedly cursed by a priest, to bring death to anyone who wishes to use it for greed.

—*Legends and Lore of Famous Stones*

I spent a solid 90 minutes with the two older women, feeling the tensions of work, life, everything just drain away. The coffee was bland, the cakes a little dry, but it was the company I wanted. After a while, however, the warmth and comfort of the sitting room made me feel sleepier and sleepier. I kissed them both and headed off.

I'd reserved a room in a hotel close to the top of the town. It turned out to be an agreeable old house, with heavy paneling on the walls and pressed curtains at the windows of the foyer. The smell of meat and onions hung in the air from the restaurant/pub on the ground floor as I checked in. I'd have a nice shower then find something sustaining, which is never hard to find in Scotland. Honestly, with all the bakeries with their fluffy white breads and delicate cakes, with the brideys and bacon rolls, you'd think the whole country would be rolling around like little butterballs, but they're not. It's a sturdy population, plain-faced and direct, with dogs and people taking their exercise outside all the time.

In my plain, pleasing room, I tipped the busboy, a youth of maybe seventeen with a shaved head and a thick earring in his left lobe, and threw my suitcase on the bed. I kicked off my shoes, and started unbuttoning my blouse as I headed for the bathroom to start the shower. Another reason to have a room in a hotel. Showers have never particularly caught on in homes in Britain. It's better than it was when I was a child, but still a long way from the copious amounts of high pressure water you get in America.

As I shed my blouse, jet lag started kicking in again, thick along the back of my neck, weighting my eyelids, making my shoulders ache. I glanced at the clock: 6:17. To get on schedule, I would have to stay up until at least 9:30.

At the moment, it seemed impossible.

Steam curled out of the bathroom. I stripped as I went, leaving a trail from bed to bathroom. Sheer white blouse, bra, red leather skirt—I have a penchant for leather—panties. My skin felt sweaty and sticky, and the water was heaven. The toiletries were high-end, smelling of lavender. For one second, as the spray massaged my back, I thought with some pleasure of the possibility of my Continental, with his long, clean hands. Hands on my tired neck would be very nice indeed. He'd seemed charming enough, and it wouldn't be so bad to have a holiday affair, especially given the anniversary of my divorce.

But I didn't want to mix family into it. I'd chosen the Drover pub because no one I knew was likely to be there. It's not always possible, but I keep family and love life, as well as business and love life, strictly separated.

Business is obvious. It's too hard to work with someone you've slept with and dumped or been dumped by.

And the trouble with families is that they always hope you're going to settle down. That's not on my agenda. Tried marriage for three years, and really, not married is better. Men are too unreliable. I should have learned that from my father's example, but it took a bad marriage—with a man so much like my father they might have been clones; that is, handsome, charming, and completely incapable of fidelity—to drive the truth all the way home.

So I stood alone under the hot shower, washing the breath of hundreds of other people from my long hair, scrubbing the layers of grime from my face.

Feeling better, I wrapped one towel around my head and another around my body. Stepping over the clothes on the floor, I unzipped my black carry-on to get out some lotion and deodorant, mentally trying to choose between jeans and a skirt to wear downstairs.

It took ten full seconds to sink in: this was not my bag.

It was an exact replica, which isn't so weird—how many black, wheeled carry-on models are there, after all?—but in the netted pocket where I keep my underwear, there were boxer shorts. Instead of my prized red leather pants, there was a stack of neatly folded T-shirts.

"Damn!"

I put my hand on the straps, lifted the edge of a blue shirt as if it were a false front, a little practical joke, and just below it, I'd find my own things. How could this have happened? I'd had it with me all the way from California!

But obviously, that wasn't true, or I wouldn't be looking at some man's things instead of my own.

Think. Where could it have been mixed up? It

could have happened when I pulled the bag out of the overhead bin. Not likely. I wedged it next to the right-hand wall, and took it down from the same spot.

Where else then? At security. I suppose I could have grabbed the wrong bag off the belt.

Except my shoes were in the bin right next to it.

Which left the van I used to get to the airport. I thought back to the other passengers, wondering which one might be opening my bag with the same sinking feeling I had right now.

There were three men. One was too fat to wear these clothes, one was a college boy and one was a pin-striped, red-tie business man who'd smelled of my father's Armani cologne. He might wear silk boxers, but I didn't see him in a turquoise linen shirt. I fingered it with admiration. Silk and linen, gorgeously cut. I'd like to see the man who'd wear this.

Probably not the van, then. Maybe it was the security check point. But I hadn't paid any attention to who was around me there. I'd been running late.

"Damn!" I said again.

I didn't *want* to wear my dirty plane-ride clothes. I wanted something that smelled clean. I wanted my nightgown to sleep in. My other shoes.

But there wasn't anything I could do, except track down the owner of the case and try to work out an exchange. In the meantime, I'd have to go shopping in the morning.

I found a tag in a small pocket on the outside of the bag. Same place mine was, of course. The handwriting was hard to read, spidery and European. I couldn't make out the name, which was smeared, but there was a telephone number, in Paris.

Paris. Dialing the numbers gave me a jolt of body memory, one of those electric moments that are stored God knows where, in cells all over your arms or back or collarbone or ankles. This particular memory, dialing Paris numbers, had been imprinted during my seventeenth year, when I'd dialed the number of a man, a Parisian who'd stolen my heart with a single kiss.

So I thought I was just projecting when the recorded voice on the other end sounded exactly like the voice of that very man, Paul Maigny. In French he said, "Hello, thank you for calling, please leave a message."

Startled, I hung up. Stared at the phone, the card in a hand that had suddenly begun to tremble violently.

It couldn't be Paul, of course. Only someone who sounded like him. Paul still lived in Paris—my father, his best friend, had recently spent a week with him— but I would have known if he'd been on that plane. With a slight shake of my head, I picked up the receiver and dialed again. Again the voice shocked me.

And again, before I could decide what to do, I hung up.

There are some voices you do not forget. Your

mother. Your best friend. Your spouse. I was not mistaken about this one, either. Those elegant vowels, the slight rasp.

I scowled.

It had been almost five years since I'd heard Paul's voice—since the day of my wedding, as a matter of fact, when I'd told him never to speak to me again. And he was likely in my mind because the island of Arran, lying backward on the sea like a man, made me think of him. Still.

It couldn't be his case on my bed. I knew it wasn't his handwriting, which was an elegant, sprawling hand I'd seen thousands of times.

I was just imagining things.

Firmly, I dialed the number a third time. When the voice mail picked up, I left my name and the telephone number of the hotel on the voice mail of the stranger in Paris, who no doubt had my bag and felt as bewildered as I did. In case he'd left a message for me, I next dialed my home voice mail box. No messages.

So there I was, damp in my towels, with a hot date in an hour. The stranger's bag was open on the bed. I did what any red-blooded woman would do: I looked through it. Maybe there would be something I could wear.

A scent of laundry and man rose from it, entirely alien from the smell of my own packing. I wondered, briefly, if the stranger would go through my things. I thought of thongs and red leather pants—when you have a job as stuffy as mine, you've got to take your pleasure where you can find it—and a little sense of discomfort rippled through me.

Beyond the gorgeous turquoise silk and linen shirt, there was a black, zipped shaving kit, three silk T-shirts, a pair of black trousers, black socks, a pair of well-worn jeans, swimming trunks, the aforementioned boxers. A pair of walking sandals were sealed in a plastic bag. A little sand gathered in the corner. He'd been on the beach.

My stomach growled and it hit me again that I was starving. Which brought home the fact that I still I didn't have anything to wear.

Grr. All I'd wanted was a little supper and a good night's sleep. The mix-up was a pain in the neck.

But let's get a grip here—it was not tragedy or disaster. It was only inconvenient. I keep some makeup in my purse, and the hair dryer in the bathroom would work fine for my wet head.

What I didn't have was deodorant. With only a slight flush of shame, I opened the man's shaving kit to see if he had any. There it was, a red roll-on that smelled pretty good.

There was also a white box. Jewelry, I thought—after all, jewels are my stock in trade—I opened it to see what taste he had on this level. Judging by the rest of it, it would be something understated. Probably gold, expensive.

It was expensive, all right.

For the second time in five minutes, my brain couldn't get itself around what my eyes were seeing. It wasn't a watch or a ring or even a tacky bracelet.

Pillowed in cotton batting was a jewel. A diamond.

A *huge* diamond.

My hands shook as I pulled it out. Not only was it huge, it was very rare and storied, this jewel. A jewel that was presumed to be lost. It was very old. Priceless.

It was even cursed.

Katerina's Blood.

Since I was one of only a handful of people who would recognize the astonishment of it at first sight, I was also convinced of one other thing.

The switch of bags was not an accident.

# Chapter 4

Many stones are valued for their rarity; for example, the colored stones, rubies, sapphires and emeralds are rated on their scarcity. In spite of public perception, diamonds are not among the rare stones on the earth. They're plentiful the world over, and if it were not for a cartel controlling the distribution of these sparkling stones, the cost of diamonds would be much lower.

—Sylvie Montague, *Ancient Jewels and the Modern World*

Jewel geeks are an odd little club. We come to it in many ways, from many walks in life. My entry came through a trip to the British Museum when I was eleven, when a family friend took me to see the crown jewels. There I saw a collection of Indian Raj's jewels and was stung right through the chest. In that instant, I fell madly in love with the entire mythology and wonder of gems. I have been handling them, assessing them, admiring them in my work professionally for eight years, and have seen some spectacular beauties. My particular specialty—passion—is for ancient and antique jewels.

The Katerina made my heart race. I carried it to the window, as carefully as if it were a baby bird, and held it up to the light.

Good grief.

The diamond was legendary, its history vague— very, very famous, but also elusive, changing hands with dizzying speed. I couldn't remember the exact weight off the top of my head, but I knew it was something over 80 karats. As a point of reference, the Hope Diamond is 43.

Katerina's Blood was cut in medieval times, so it wasn't the glittery, winking faceted one of more modern diamonds. It was what they call table cut, flat across the top, with two narrow facets along each side. Laid in a brooch, it was set in white gold, with a line of pigeon's blood rubies encircling it. The color was nearly crystal, clear without yellow or brown to mar it. In the diamond business, it would be a grade D, nearly as clear as glass.

But it was neither the size nor the extraordinary color that made this diamond so very, very famous and prized. It was a flaw.

Most diamonds have what are called inclusions— bits of other stones or dust or other flaws that mar the clarity of the jewel. Usually such flaws render diamonds much less valuable, but the "flaw" in Katerina's Blood was a ruby. It floated like a drop of blood in the center of the stone.

As long as I could remember, I'd heard of this possibility—and had often heard of the gem—but the reality was beyond even my wildest imaginings.

It was unbelievably beautiful. I could barely breathe with the wonder of it. One of the rarest, most storied jewels in the world. In my hand. All the history, all the people who'd held it, all the tragedies attached to it—

The phone rang. My reverence shattered so violently that I dropped the Katerina. It banged against my toe and bounced across the rug. The phone rang again. I grabbed the diamond and headed across the room with shaking hands, thinking it must be the person who had my—

Oh, God.

A foot from the table, I stopped. Clutched the jewel to my chest.

It *had* been Paul on that answering machine in Paris. Some coincidences in life I could buy—say, watching a movie then seeing an actor from it at a local restaurant, or maybe Halley's Comet streaking by on my birthday.

I could not swallow the notion that somehow, by accident, I held in my hands the jewel Paul Maigny had most wished—all of his life—to see and touch. His father, a jewel thief of some talent, had died trying to attain it. Paul, who had, in turn, fostered my own passion for jewels, had spoken of the Katerina to me many, many times.

I clutched the jewel, narrowed my eyes at the phone, as if it were responsible for this mess.

What was going on here? Paul was a collector and aficionado, not a thief like his father. The Katerina would be a gem he would pursue with great passion if he knew it had surfaced.

But he would not deliberately involve me. Which meant that someone else had learned of my connection to Paul, and planned to use me to get to him, or use me as protection against him.

The phone shrilled again. I had no doubt it was Paul on the other end. My mentor, my father's best friend, at one time my guardian, and a man I had once believed I loved more than anyone on earth.

I let the phone ring.

I told myself it was because I was going to be damned sure I knew what the hell was going on. I wanted to know who stole it, where it had been, why I had been chosen to carry it here to Ayr.

The ring shrilled. I thought of the last time I'd seen Paul, before my wedding in San Francisco. I thought of picking up the receiver, listening to whatever he'd say.

Instead, I just stood there.

The phone stopped ringing. With slightly shaky hands, I gathered my clothes from the floor. There were spare undies in my purse, and I shimmied into them, then the skirt I'd worn on the plane. The blouse was crumpled and sweaty. Ditto the bra. I thought about going without, but that would be my hiding place, so I had to put it on. The jewel, long and flat, slipped into the space below my left breast. In the mirror, I looked to see if it was obvious, but the blouse draped down loosely, and unless a person touched it, no one would ever notice.

From the suitcase, I took out the silk and linen shirt—payment for my troubles—and it was as luscious against my skin as I'd imagined. It was clean, but I could smell a hint of the man in it. Paul? I didn't think this was his smell.

By then, I started to feel jumpy. Nervous. Had the jewel been part of the cache taken from the drug honcho? Or had it come from some other source? How could I find out?

A rumble rolled loudly through my belly, and a jet-lag headache was pounding against my sinus. Adrenaline had perked me up, but in order to think clearly, I would really need some sleep. First, food.

I'd work out a more detailed plan later, but for now, I'd go ahead and meet the guy from the plane— it occurred to me that I didn't even know his name yet—and eat, then come back and get some sleep. In the morning, I'd ring the Glasgow police and do some fishing. In the meantime, I'd keep it to myself. The fewer people in the loop, the better.

Maybe I'd ring my father, too, if I could figure out where he was staying and under what name. I'd check the race schedule first, to be sure he wasn't in the middle of the Grand Prix. No point in worrying him if he was driving. He'd done very well last year, and there was talk that he was making a comeback, that he might be the one to unseat Michael Schumacher at last.

If the race hadn't started, I could innocently probe him about Paul.

My hair was just damp, and rather than taking time to dry it, I wove it into a braid that hung against my spine. I examined myself in the mirror. The diamond did not show.

The phone rang again. I grabbed my purse and coat and rushed out without answering. A creepy sense of urgency crawled down my neck, the same warning that shows up when I'm driving some-times—a sharp directive I've learned to obey. This one said, *Get out, get out!* I did. I was on the high street in three minutes.

It was early evening, still light, and there were

plenty of people out walking. Too dark for sunglasses, and I had not thought to bring a hat. I was worried that I might bump into someone I knew—a cousin or a neighbor of a relative—and they'd want to join me, and then I'd have to say no, and then there would be hurt feelings all around. Plus, until I could figure out what was going on, I really didn't want to take the chance that this business might put somebody in danger. Besides me, anyway.

I really wished I hadn't stopped at my grandmother's house.

I kept my head down. The street was busier than I would have expected for mid-March. There were tourists around, mixing with the matrons in their cardigans, plaid skirts and sensible shoes, teenagers with piercings and their shaved heads. It all made me very aware of both my jet lag and my empty stomach, which now roared in response to the smell of meat and onions in the air. I paused for a minute, looking around.

And damned if I didn't see my cousin Keith three doors down. Luckily, he was talking on a cell phone and didn't see me. I ducked behind a crowd of Australian schoolteacher-types and followed them into the pub. I found a seat in the dark back room, ordered a pint of Stella and the most ordinary meal in the world—pie, beans and chips—and tried to figure out what my next moves should be.

The jukebox played old rock and roll quietly. At

the bar sat a gathering of after-work males. The sound of their voices—that lilting accent, always the sound of my mother—eased the tension in the back of my neck. I took the first big breath I'd had in a half hour.

Beneath my left breast was the comforting bulk of the diamond. Who had made sure I got it? Why?

As if called by my questions, the man from the airport materialized at the end of the room. He stood there, staring straight at me, for a minute. No longer smiling, and I didn't know if it was the light or my fresh knowledge, but he looked older and a lot more dangerous than he had sleeping over the Atlantic.

The certainty penetrated my jet-lag fog: he, too, had a part in this.

I knew he was too good too be true. I cursed myself for being attracted to him anyway.

He approached and gestured toward the empty seat in front of me. "May I?"

I just looked at him. He sat down, and I realized he was older than I first thought—early- to mid-thirties instead of a decade younger. The bartender came over and he ordered a pint.

The bartender nodded. "Want something to eat?"

"I ordered the pie," I said.

He nodded. "Another then."

When the bartender was gone, the man took off his leather coat and rubbed a hand across his face. "Pssh," he said, and leaned on his elbows. Even in the darkened room, his eyes were astonishing, like chips of blue marble. Looking at the shirt I'd taken from the suitcase, he said, "My sister bought me that shirt in Paris. It's my favorite."

"I'm keeping it for my troubles."

His gaze slid admiringly down my body, over my breasts. Somehow—I don't know why—a European man can almost always get away with that, while it's only the rare American who can. His eyes came back to my face. Direct contact, eye to eye.

He had those beautifully cut lips, a slight grizzling of black beard. Good hands. You can tell a lot about a man by the way he moves his hands. An old boy-friend of mine used to just barely scratch the top of a cat's head. It was frustrating. Guess what else was frustrating?

"It suits you," he said. It took me a moment to realize he meant the shirt.

"Thanks," I said, then shook my head. "Let's not play games, all right. You need to tell me what's going on. Who are you? And what is this really about?"

He leaned back to let the bartender set down his pint. Waited until he was gone before he said, "You found it, then?"

"A little hard to miss."

A slight inclination of his chin, not quite a nod. "And you have it?"

I gave him a look. "What do you think?"

"Good."

"Where are my things?"

He drunk from his glass of beer, thirstily. "I have your bag in my car."

"I was furious about my leather pants. Do have any idea how much they cost?"

"I have good reasons to involve you, I swear it."

"Where does Paul Maigny come into it?"

The heavy lashes swept down for a minute. Good. He wasn't a total fool if he was smart enough to be afraid of Maigny. "May I tell you after we eat? It would be safer." He glanced over his shoulder. "Maybe we can take a little walk on the beach, eh?"

If I hadn't been so bloody starving, I'd have insisted we go right then, but there was nothing to be gained by skipping a meal that would be served any minute. "All right. Maybe in the meantime, you can tell me your name. You already know mine."

"Luca Colceriu."

"What do you do?"

One eyebrow lifted elegantly. "That's saved for later."

I lifted my beer and took a slow sip. A burly man with a receding hairline walked to the jukebox and put in some coins. "Well, then, what shall we talk about, Mr. Colceriu?"

"Do you know the legend of this jewel?"

"Bits and pieces," I said. "Not the whole thing.

Something about a prince, and curse." I almost touched the comforting solidness of it beneath my blouse and resisted. It was there.

"It was discovered in India, in medieval times," Luca said. "A Romanian prince—"

"Ah-ha. Romanian. Of course."

He looked confused. "Pardon me?"

I shook my head. "I couldn't place your accent earlier. Romanian, of course."

"Right."

"Anyway, on with the story."

Looking a little bewildered, Luca continued. "Yes, well, the prince purchased it and had it made into a splendid necklace for his wife-to-be."

"Katerina."

"Yes. Three days after he gave it to her, she was gruesomely murdered by the prince's rivals. The prince, in his grief, ordered her buried with the gem around her throat, and then he killed himself. His younger brother took the throne."

A jewel that had been buried in a grave now pressed into my left breast. Even with my passion for stones, that was a little unnerving. "Eww."

He raised an eyebrow.

Our food came, two heavy white plates of plain Scottish pub fare. It smelled heavenly—like onions, like meat and fat and a thousand blipping memories of my mother. I picked up my fork and took a deep breath before digging into the beans. "Perfect," I said.

He followed suit, without my reverence, and nodded. "Not bad."

"Back to the jewel," I prompted. "Someone must have done some grave-robbing, however, because it's not down there around her neck anymore, is it?"

He took his time, then in his slightly formal English said, "It was two generations before enough of the curse had ebbed for people not to be afraid of it. A greedy priest, with his eye on the papacy, twisted church law for a new prince to dig it up, retrieve the jewel." He took a bite of pie, washed it down with beer. "The priest was killed by a lunatic three days later, a leper who'd lost his mind and killed three others before he was restrained."

I scowled, and maybe it was my imagination, but it suddenly felt the jewel was very hot against my skin. "What about the prince who ordered it dug up?"

"I do not know about him."

There are some things worth enjoying, and food was one of them. Despite the weird circumstances, the danger, the jewel, I was determined to enjoy my first Scottish meal in nearly five years. Hot food. Good food. Heaven. "I guess mass murder isn't a new thing after all, huh?"

His teeth flashed, white and square. The grin lightened his whole face, and I could suddenly see through to someone else, a man who made jokes in a language I didn't understand, to friends he'd known his whole life, who all lived a life entirely different from my own.

I wanted, suddenly, to go back with him to his Romanian world, into a walk-up flat in a faceless post-war building. I could see the kitchen, Communist-built utilitarian and plain, with half curtains at the window. There would be a little television on a stand on which he watched football games. The kind of football where they wore shorts, not shoulder pads.

It lasted only a flash, my little vision, but it must have put a different expression on my face, because his shifted. His gaze was more direct, his mouth softer in that way that's so dangerous for a woman who has been devastated by the games of men. "What do you know, Sylvie Montague? Hmm?"

I looked away, lifted a shoulder. "Don't even start playing with me," I said, and looked back. "And don't make the mistake of underestimating me. You'll regret it."

"I will not underestimate you." His mouth lifted on one side, and he held up one hand. "Promise."

"Finish the story," I said.

"Well, it goes on as it began. A murder over and over, whenever someone got his hands on it. It is stolen, disappears for a generation or two, resurfaces."

"So not everyone who comes into contact with it dies."

"No."

"But you're not taking any chances, are you?"

He lifted a brow. "I am a thief. Perhaps not the cleanest soul, yes?" His eyes glittered. "I prefer not to touch it."

"It's okay if I'm cursed to possible murder? Thanks ever so."

"You do not believe in curses."

"I wouldna count on that," I said in my best Scottish English. I drank a deep draft of my beer. "I am half Scot myself, you know. We believe in the dark side."

"Not you," he said, and his voice was quite sure.

I scowled. "What makes you think you know me?"

He leaned forward, elbows on the table. "You don't believe in anything. You don't believe in ghosts or God or curses." His eyes were steady. "Men, families, nothing."

A hollowness emptied out my chest. I narrowed my eyes. "You did your research."

He tilted his head. Curls tumbled to one side. "Yes."

Against my thigh, my cell phone buzzed suddenly. It startled me, but I grabbed it and looked at the ID to see who was calling in. "Unknown" flashed over the screen. That might have meant it was anyone at all in Scotland, since I didn't have their numbers programmed in. I didn't answer.

"Sorry," I said, "I have relatives here. That's something you might have considered, you know, before you dumped you *secret* on me."

"I did."

A brief cold chill touched the back of my neck. "What does that mean?"

He shrugged. "Nothing. Just that you'd have resources."

"For...?"

"To help you, that's all. You do not think I would hurt them?" He said it with a slight shake of his head, a slight wrinkling of his brow.

I met his gaze, smiled slightly. "Luca, don't try to play me. I was raised with international playboys and the women who wanted their money, with thieves and art experts and people currying for favor with every sort of celebrity you can imagine." I narrowed my eyes. "You're an amateur."

For a long moment, everything about him was utterly still, and I had a clear image of a sleek cat, tail twitching dangerously.

Then the thick black lashes swept down, heat rose in his cheeks, and he laughed softly. "Forgive me." His chin jutted out, and he met my gaze. "I forgot who raised you."

"Touché," I said, heat in my own cheeks. I slammed down the rest of my pint. "Let's get out of here. You can get me my suitcase."

I stood, jammed my arms into my coat sleeves. He

stood with me, and put his hand on my arm. His hair gave off a scent of cloves and oranges, startling and exotic. "Sylvie, I am sorry."

"I'm going to the toilet." I pulled my arm away, tossed my purse over my shoulder. "Pay for our dinner. Then you can tell me what the hell is going on."

"I will," he said, taking out his wallet. "I promise."

# Chapter 5

The first step in evaluating a diamond is the simplest, *cut*. There are eight basic cuts for a diamond: emerald, heart, pear, round, marquise, radiant, oval and princess. There are others, of course, but these are the main shapes found in modern diamonds.

—www.costellos.com.au

In the ladies' room, I checked my lipstick and then took out my phone. One message was waiting, and I flipped open the phone to punch in the voice mail number. Nothing happened. The phone flipped back to the original icon of a flashing envelope. I tried it a second time, and the same thing happened.

I scowled, but I'd have time to figure it out later. I washed my hands and went back out front. Luca was counting out money to the bartender. While I waited for him, a short, sturdy-looking man at the bar said, "Hey, ain't you that race car driver's daughter? The one in papers all the time?"

I raised my brows. "'Fraid so."

"Yer mum's a local girl? I went to grammar school with her."

"Is that right?" I smiled. "I'm here to visit my grandmother."

"She was sweet, yer mum. I was wrecked to hear what happened to her."

"Thanks." Against my hip, my phone buzzed again, and I was about to pull it out when Luca came toward me, tucking pound coins in his jeans pocket. Time enough to check the message later—it was likely a cousin or aunt, anyway.

"Take care," I said to the man at the bar.

"You do the same, gerl."

Luca went out on the street into the dusk, but I remembered in time to duck my head out first and look for my cousin Keith, who'd been out here just a little while ago. No sign of him. No sign of anyone much, really. I stepped out. A small breeze buffeted my bare knees, and it would be cold later, but it wasn't bad yet.

"Which way?" I said to Luca.

"A car park by the station," he said, cocking his thumb. "Will you walk with me for a little while first, please? Let me tell you my story?"

A damp gloaming hung in the air, soft purple brushed with orange, and I did want to walk by the sea before I slept. *This* sea, which I'd traveled a very long way to visit. Birds with muscular wings flapped overhead, calling to their mates to come get supper amid the pools left behind by the tide. I could smell the muskiness of the water.

Beside me, Luca stood a head taller than I, his body lean and graceful, his shoulders a square evenness I wanted to touch. He tossed on a leather jacket, and I found my gaze lingering on his mouth again.

At the same time, I was aware that he'd used me, that he was a thief, that his life was not the sort I should get mixed up in.

But how boring would life be if we only did what was good for us? "All right," I said. "It better be good."

"That will be for you to decide."

I tucked my purse close and folded my arms over my chest as we headed west, down the street toward the sea. "You stole the jewel?" I prompted.

"Yes," he said. "I am, by profession, a thief."

"And where did it come from?"

He smiled slightly as we emerged onto the quiet

promenade. "I imagined you had unraveled that by now."

"Ah. The Kingpin. The drug lord." I paused at the top of a short set of steps to the sand. The last fingers of light gave a backlight to the Goat Fells on Arran, and splashed against the windows of the expensive homes lining the beach.

Luca inclined his head. "You do not know who it is?"

"Who? You mean the drug lord?"

"Yes. They called him The Swede."

"Doesn't ring a bell. Should I know it?"

"Perhaps. It will explain the Maigny connection."

I waited, but he was savoring his moment. I spread my hands. "Well?"

"Henrik Gunnarsson."

"Still nothing," I said. "And while I know Maigny would not particularly care for a close examination of his business, I wouldn't think drugs would appeal to him." He preferred art, jewels, antiques. "Drugs would be too messy."

"Let's walk," Luca said, gesturing.

I frowned at his stalling, and stopped where I stood. Wind came off the water, brisk and invigorating, but it would soon be very cold. The wind skittered up my skirt and I shivered. "Let's not. We can stand here on the bridge."

"As you wish." He faced the sea, putting his face in profile, and I saw something ancient in the Semitic angle of his high-bridged nose, the fullness of his lips. A profile meant for an ancient Greek coin. No, not Greek. An ancient Romanian coin. Yes, that worked. A Gypsy prince, that was Luca, both wild and elegant. The wind gusted his scent of oranges toward me, and I found myself breathing it in before I knew what I was doing.

Dangerous.

In a hard voice, I said, "Tell me."

"Maigny hired me to steal the jewel from Gunnarsson. They are old, old rivals—something that began over a woman who became Maigny's mistress. You may remember her."

"He had a lot of mistresses," I said with a shrug.

"I have the impression this one might have meant a little more to him. Elena?"

I didn't say anything, but memories swished forward. A woman with a deep bust and long legs and beautiful shoes, chuckling at me. A man with ice-blond hair and cool eyes, smoking on a balcony in Paris. Paul, his jaw hard, ordering them out of his house. I couldn't have been more than twelve or thirteen. "I remember her, but not because he was so madly in love." Though I supposed he might have been. What did I know—or care—of adult love affairs at the time? "She betrayed him. Stole something, maybe. I can't remember exactly."

"Yes, she betrayed him. She stole a Celtic brooch from him, and took it to Gunnarsson."

"I see." And I could. I could imagine the cold fury that must have overtaken him when he discovered her treachery. "So, how did Gunnarsson end up with the Katerina?"

"It was largely to thwart Maigny," Luca said.

"Ah." Old, bad blood. How typical of men. "So Paul wanted it as payback for the earlier theft." It was a test to see how much he knew.

He glanced at me below his lashes, quick and measuring. "Not exactly. Partly, of course, but he has been seeking this jewel for twenty years or better. Something to do with his father." He shrugged, and leaning on the bridge, laced his hands together. "I don't know."

"His father was a thief, like you," I said. I watched a pair of gulls wheeling against the eggplant-colored sky. "He spent years tracking down the Katerina, and managed to at last steal it from a war criminal who'd fled to Brazil. Paul was young, eight or nine, and saw the jewel when his father brought it home."

"Mmm." Luca's murmur was sympathetic—and knowing. "I can guess the next part. Maigny's father was murdered and the jewel disappeared."

"From what I gather, it was quite brutal. Dismemberment, maybe even decapitation."

Was it my imagination or did Luca shudder slightly? "So it goes with curses."

I thought of Gunnarsson, he of the Kingpin's

Crown Jewels that I'd been brought in to evaluate. He'd been garroted. "Did you know the Kingpin?"

"No." The word was short and cold. "He was dead before I arrived. He had only held the Katerina three days."

"And was murdered."

He looked down at me, his hands quiet on the stone balustrade of the bridge. "Yes."

"Who did it?"

"Who knows? Perhaps it was your Maigny."

"No." Paul was a very wealthy man with an eye for beauty who'd made his fortune in canny investments. While I could credit the idea of his hiring a thief to steal a gem from a drug lord with whom he had an old grievance, I didn't think he was a killer. "Who else wanted the jewel?"

He made a pishing noise. "More to the point, who did not?"

I nodded. "And you have now stolen it yourself."

"Yes."

"Has he paid you?"

"Half."

I raised my eyebrows. "And now you've stolen it and have his cash and there are others after the jewel, and if you live another week it will be a miracle." I tossed my heavy braid over my shoulder. "And you dragged me into this mess, why?"

"It belongs to Romania," he said.

I half snorted. "And a thief cares about that, why?"

He gave me an injured look. "My country is poor but proud, and she has been overlooked. Our wealth comes in claiming our own heritage and taking pride in it. If the crown jewels of England were stolen, wouldn't a British thief wish to return them?"

"I suppose." I was still picking up a note of insincerity. Something not quite right. A gust tossed handfuls of dust into my eyes. "Let's go back." We turned around, and I noticed a pair of lovers kissing on a bench. Something about them looked—off.

I frowned. Or was I just being paranoid? Not everybody was paparazzi. "What do I have to do with all of this?"

"Your name was in the newspapers after the murder."

"Yeah. And?"

He paused, put his hand on my arm. Again the night wind blew his exotic scent toward me, mixing it with the sea in a heady combination. I looked at his mouth, wondered...

"When I saw your photo in the paper, I knew I had seen it before, but only when they mentioned your father was Gordon Montague did I realize that I could protect myself from Paul's wrath."

I raised an eyebrow. "How will I protect you?"

"Sylvie, think," he said. "Why choose you? He won't kill me as long as you are with me."

"Why would I care if he kills you?"

"It does not matter what you think. It matters that he will do nothing to endanger you. You are the most precious of all creatures to him, did you know that?"

I snorted. "We haven't spoken in five years."

"That may be," he said quietly, and lifted a hand to my face to capture a strand of long hair that had escaped my braid. He smoothed it back. "But it has not changed his feelings for you. He's very protective of you."

Luca's fingers were graceful and delicate on my cheekbone, and as I looked up at him warily, I spied something in his blue eyes. Surprise, perhaps. A tendril of awareness unfurled on my spine as he took a step closer.

From behind us came a shout, "Hey, Sylvie! Is that your new boyfriend?"

I turned, instinctively, and the flashes went off, pop, pop.

"Shit." I whirled away, putting my back to them. "C'mon," I said to Luca. "Let's get out of here."

He had not moved, his hand still circling my arm. He appeared to be confused as he stared at the photographers, and I'm sure they caught very flattering, open-mouthed pictures of him. They'd run with some appropriately awful headline about shocking secrets or something appropriately comic-bookish.

The flashes from the cameras lit up the night, and Luca scowled. "Who—?"

"Fucking paparazzi," I said, striding away. "Where's the car?"

He hurried to catch me. "Language, language," he said with a chuckle in his voice.

"You try having sleazy photographers taking your picture every time you're about to kiss someone." I was still stinging from an encounter in New York last spring, when the doggedness of a pair of photographers had cost me a developing relationship with a man I'd really liked. Joseph had been a professor at Berkley. He'd found the attention daunting, and dumped me.

"Were we about to kiss?" Luca asked.

I glared at him. "Don't be arch."

He grinned. "The car is here." He pointed toward a car park near the train station. Behind us the photographers strolled along, shooting photos lazily, their cigarette smoke carried invisibly toward us on the night.

He led the way toward a tiny Ford Mini. White. I raised an eyebrow. "Could you *possibly* have chosen anything less cool?"

He made a face, brushed the question from the air with a wave of his hand, and opened the passenger door for me. There was that one moment of disorientation when I looked down and there was no steering wheel on the left. I started to duck into the car, but Luca captured my arm. Stopped me.

And before I knew what was happening, he slid his

hand into my hair, tilted his head toward mine and kissed me.

Even as I was falling into it, I knew exactly what he was doing—for some reason he wanted our photos in the tabloids. He wanted something passionate and sexy. Under ordinary circumstances, I'd never be famous enough to make the covers, but with the news of the drug dealer's stash, and the sexy possibility of a lost gem, and the excitement over my father's current wins on the circuit, chances were excellent— especially with Luca's good looks—that we'd be plastered over them all tomorrow. For a split second, I wondered who he wanted to see us.

I started to pull back, half offended, but who was I kidding? I was using him, too. It wouldn't exactly kill me to have my ex-husband see photos of me kissing some dashing foreigner. For a single long moment, I felt a ripple of satisfaction at the idea of Timothy standing in line in some grocery store, and the tabloids emblazoned with me and Luca kissing.

That was where I was in one minute.

The very next second, he lifted his head slightly, his hands cupped around my face, and he looked faintly puzzled. "Well," he whispered, and before I could gather my senses enough to move away, he'd bent his head again, claimed my mouth, and some- thing shifted with both of us.

Just that simple. He tasted exactly right. There are

people you know are bad for you and you let them get away with murder for all kinds of physical reasons. That's all I can tell you about Luca. His mouth was as luscious as it looked, the lips full and delicious and somehow elegant. That scent of oranges, sharp as freshly grated peel, swept through me, made my hips soft, and I lost my head for three seconds.

Or maybe it was thirty.

I know my head fell back into his palm, that his thumb was on my cheek, that he might have been mugging for the cameras at first, but it shifted for him at the same instant it did for me, and there was nothing pretend in the sudden thrust of his tongue, the sparking electricity that ran in blue rivulets between us. That tendril of unfurling awareness on my spine moved trough my body, twining around those places our bodies touched—chest, knees, lips.

I very nearly let go. His fingers slid down my neck, traced my collarbone—

Some internal alarm screamed my name. I shoved him away. "Stop!"

For one long second, he didn't release me, only hovered there a moment, eyes sharp and hot, one hand still tangled in my hair. His lips were slightly parted. I forgot there were photographers hovering. Forgot that I had a giant diamond stashed in my bra. Forgot I was in Scotland for a good reason and I needed to protect my integrity.

Then his nostrils flared and he abruptly dropped his hands, moved away from me.

"Get in," he said.

# Chapter 6

Diamonds were worn by aristocratic families to ward off the plague during the Middle Ages. The poorest people always died first, since they lived closer to the docks, where the ships often brought the plague from other countries. The rich had an idea that since the poor went first, that displaying their wealth (diamonds) would keep them from infection.

—Margaret Odrowaz-Sypniewski, B.F.A.

When I climbed into the car, he slammed the door and came around to get behind the wheel. He did not

look at me as he turned the key in the ignition. I
noticed that his hands were shaking slightly.

"Where is your room?" he asked gruffly.

I gave him directions. He nearly turned the wrong
way out of the parking lot, and cursed left-hand drive
before he corrected his turn. "When will Britain catch
up with the rest of the world on traffic?"

"Never."

"It's idiotic."

I shrugged. "Probably."

It took longer to get out of the parking lot than it
did to get to the hotel, and we pulled up into the lot
there. Lamplight glowed at the windows stacked up
into the darkness.

Would I invite him in? Under other circumstances,
I might have. But I would not do it tonight. There
were too many volatilities built into it. Too much at
stake.

I got out. He followed me, keys in hand, to the back
of the car. Without speaking, he opened the trunk, let
me grab my bag, and slammed the top down again.

"Thanks," I said, and headed toward the door of the
hotel, rolling the case behind me. He followed.

I stopped. "What are you doing?"

"Coming with you."

"Why?"

"What are you going to do, Sylvie?" He scowled.
"Turn it in to the authorities?"

That was exactly what I *should* do. My career depended on my doing exactly that. Why was I hesitating? "I don't know yet."

"Before you act, Sylvie, will you think on it? It belongs to Romania. If you take it to Maigny, it will never be there again."

"He has no part in this. I told you, we haven't spoken in years."

"So you say." He paused. "If you will help me return it to Romania, I will make it worth your while."

"If I do that, my career is over, Luca."

"Not if it appears that I kidnapped you."

I shook my head. "No."

He lowered his eyes, then looked at me. "And what if I kidnap you now?"

"You would have done it already if that was what you intended." I paused with my hand on the door to the hotel. "Would have been much easier for you all around, wouldn't it? Grab me in San Francisco, make sure Paul knew so he didn't kill you and then get the jewel back to Romania."

"Yes."

I met his eyes. "But you didn't. You're a thief, but not violent."

A slight shrug. He started to speak, then paused. Looked toward the parking lot. "If—"

I waited, but he didn't finish. "'If...?'" I prompted.

"If I return the jewel to Romania, I can perhaps

regain the good opinion of my family. It would mean a great deal to me."

Something about his plea moved me. The diamond felt almost as if it started to hum against my flesh. "I'm so tired," I said. Touched cold fingers to the middle of my eyebrows. "Do you suppose we could talk about all of this in the morning?"

"Very well," he said. "Let's get my bag."

We went into the hotel, and the girl nodded to me. I went up the stairs, not wishing to wait for the tiny, narrow elevator. My room was on the third floor. Luca didn't say a word. His keys jingled in his hand as he followed behind me. It occurred to me that I should be afraid of him—but I wasn't. My instincts, honed in dozens of cities throughout my childhood spent following my father around the circuit, told me that Luca meant me no harm.

I thought of his mouth, that luscious kiss, and considered the possibility of letting him sleep in my bed tonight. And what kind of an idiot I'd be if I let him.

But you know, it had been a long bad year. My divorce anniversary was in two days. Sometimes what you want is a little affirmation that you're attractive, that you've still got it. Or maybe I just wanted the warmth of another person's skin next to mine.

On the landing, I paused. "I'm really not going to give you the jewel."

"I will not ask it." His eyes were luminous and

direct. "Take it to the police, let it be stolen again, let another fool be murdered."

"Or perhaps I'll take it to Paul," I said, dangerously.

"That, too, is an option. But a criminal who wants it for greed will surely be swept away by the curse, will he not?"

"Why would I care?"

He smiled. "Why, indeed?"

I turned my back and climbed the rest of the stairs. My door was the third one down. I paused for a second outside, and turned toward Luca. The door fell open beneath my hand, and startled, I turned back.

Holding my breath, I silently began to push it open. It was nearly impossible to keep my hand away from the priceless weight nestled beneath my left breast. The door moved heavily on well-oiled hinges, an inch at a time. There was a light on within. I couldn't remember if I'd left one on or not.

My cell phone rang.

Three things happened at once—I scrambled to pull it out of my pocket; Luca leapt forward to push the door the rest of the way open, just as someone inside the room came hurtling out. I ducked, instinctively rolling toward one side.

I shouted, "Look out!" but Luca was already down, a red gash opening over his brow. I only had a hazy impression of a burly man in a sweatshirt before I saw the gun he carried in a white, freckled hand. I dove for the floor, my cell phone ringing again. Luca was on his feet, rushing for the intruder, but the man headed straight down the hall and disappeared into another hallway, presumably stairs for the staff. Luca went after him, but returned in a moment, shaking his head. "He's gone."

The cell phone rang again, loud against my thigh. I reached for it, thinking to flip it open, but just as I got it into my hand, doors started opening along the corridor. Luca grabbed me and shoved me toward the elevator, jamming his fingers against the buttons.

I managed a muffled, "What—?"

He pulled me into him, an arm across my chest, his mouth against my ear. "We must look like lovers. Be still." He let go of a laugh, as if he were drunk, and hid the blood on his face by ducking into my shoulder.

The elevator came and he shoved me inside it. The doors closed. I yanked out of his grip, hit the second floor button. "I'm not going with you."

"They'll kill you for that jewel."

"They! Who are *they?*"

"I don't know. There were others who knew Gunnarsson had the Katerina. And someone killed him before I got there."

"This is too much," I said, putting my fingers to my temples. I desperately needed sleep, a break, some coherence.

"Sylvie, you must not be alone. Not until the jewel is delivered."

"I don't want any part of this!" I cried, and reached into my bra, yanked it out, tossed it at him. "*You* take it."

The jewel, absurdly huge, fell against the floor with a thump and lay at his feet. He literally shuddered. The elevator moved, headed downward, and he punched the stop button.

The cubicle slammed to a stop. We stood there, staring at each other, with the blood dripping down his forehead, the jewel at his feet. "Please," he said. "I will do whatever you ask. Help me."

"I don't need anything from you."

Blood trickled into his left eye and he blinked, wincing, his fingers white on the stop button. He kicked the jewel back toward me. "I am directly related to the priest who had it dug from the grave. I cannot touch it. I need you."

"You had to touch it somehow."

He shook his head. "I picked it up with a glove, put it in a box."

"You can do that now."

"Please," he said. "Help me. It is not for me. It is for Romania, for the first Katerina. For justice."

For a long moment, I thought about it. There was more I didn't know, more I wanted to understand, and it all bumped around in my head like boxes on a stormy sea. None of the story hung together. Probably a lot of that was exaggerated by the very real case of jet lag that was dragging on my brain cells.

But the one thing I did know was that I did not want to let the jewel go just this moment. Before I decided, I wanted to get some sleep. And if I were honest, didn't some part of me want to carry it to Paul himself, like an offering?

"All right," I said, and bent down to pick up the jewel. In my hand, it was startlingly alive, with a deep vibration I could feel through to my wrist. I looked at it. "It's very powerful, this stone," I said quietly.

Luca looked as if he'd throw up. "Put it away," he said.

I tucked it into my bra again, then remembered my clothes, now sitting upstairs in the hallway. "Damn it! I want to go back for my clothes."

"No," he said, adamantly.

"I have a pair of very expensive custom-made red leather pants in that bag, damn it."

"I'll buy you a new pair for God's sake. Let's go!"

# Chapter 7

*Clarity* is the next step in determining the value of a diamond. Diamonds, more than any other gemstone, have the capability to produce the maximum amount of brilliance. And a diamond that is virtually free of interior or exterior inclusions (commonly called flaws) is of the highest quality, for nothing interferes with the passage of light through the diamond. To determine a diamond's clarity, it is viewed under a 10-power magnification by a trained eye. Minute inclusions neither mar its beauty nor endanger its durability.

—www.costellos.com.au

In the parking lot, he headed toward his ridiculous little car. I shook my head. "I'm driving."

He wiped his forehead, looked at the blood smeared on his fingers. "You'd better get me a towel first."

I looked in the trunk, but it was as bare as every other rental car trunk in the world.

The pair of photographers, who'd obviously followed me to the hotel, swarmed suddenly out of the close, flashes popping. Grr. What an irritation!

"Get in the car," I barked at Luca, and followed him in. "Put something over your face."

"What? I do not have anything!"

"Use your hands, your arms. Cover the fucking blood, all right?" I turned the key. The engine rumbled to humming life, and I backed out, hit the road, letting the car have her head as we hit the open road headed south. Behind us, the photographers scrambled to follow us, but I knew they'd never catch me. Not in this car.

But they tried. They rode my tail all the way out of town.

"Are you squeamish about fast driving?" I asked.

"No."

"Good," I said, and kicked the car into a purring race, swooping around the tight curves and dark downhill drops with glee. The photographers dropped off when we sped down a six percent or so grade that whipped and turned like a test course.

Next to me, Luca was hanging on for dear life, and I laughed. "I thought it didn't frighten you?"

"I didn't know you were going to go 80 miles per hour! Holy Mother of God!"

In the rear view mirror, my tail was clean, so I dropped the speed down to a more normal level.

"Who the hell was that in my room?" I said.

"How would I know that?"

"They weren't your guys?"

"I do not have any guys, as you say it." He swore, or at least I assume it was a swear, since it was in Romanian. His fingers were pressed to his head. "I am getting blood all over me."

"Just don't get any on the car. I don't want to have to pay for cleaning."

His tone was dry. "I will do my best."

I dug in my purse and found a minipack of tissues. "Try these." When he would have tugged out just one, I shook my head. "Take out the whole thing and press it against the wound."

He did. I rounded a turn, realizing that I was headed quickly away from the lights of Ayr, my family. I looked backward into the mirror, feeling an odd sense of plucking loss.

"Do you know how long it's been since I've seen my grandmother?"

"No."

"Years. Three years."

He flicked a shoulder. "So go when we are finished here."

"Here?"

"With all this."

"You seem very sure I'll help you."

He looked at me, and it was like the moment in the pub—such a certainty about his knowledge of me that I was again unnerved. "I do not think you will turn your back on the jewel."

"I don't have any attachment to it."

"No?" He pulled the thick padding of tissue from his head, looked at it. "Perhaps I was wrong."

"That's still bleeding," I said, and downshifted as we sailed over a hill. For a brief, blissful instant, I felt the unity of car and myself. To the right was a ruin standing up against the lowering clouds. The rain was coming. I could drive forever in this elegant machine on these narrow, lonely roads with the rain coming in from the west.

I thought of the scene in the hallway of the hotel. "Who would know I have the jewel? You're the one who planted it. You must have some idea." I shifted, thinking aloud. "It had to be someone who was following you."

He turned his face toward the sea. Silent for a moment. "Probably from the drug gang, people looking for the jewel."

"Ah. Because they know it's missing and the police don't even know he had it."

"Yes."

"How did Paul know Gunnarsson had it?"

"It was on the grapevine that The Swede had purchased a very rare jewel, but Maigny didn't know until Gunnarsson sent him an e-mail."

"An e-mail," I repeated with a short laugh. "How very modern."

From the corner of my eye, I saw him gingerly exploring the wound with his finger, saw him wince. In America, we might have had a chance to find some bandages at some little shop along the road, but out here, on this rocky western coast, there would be nothing open so late save a pub that served the locals. "Does it hurt?"

A shrug.

"I'm headed for my cousin's caravan. We'll camp there tonight and figure out what to do tomorrow."

He turned his face toward me. I felt his measuring, his wondering—would we be lovers?—and did not look at him. "Don't get any ideas," I said.

"Why would I?"

"So long as we're on the same page."

He put his head back against the seat.

"I'm sure," I said, "that he has a first-aid kit there."

"No doubt." Luca closed his eyes.

The act of driving gave me a kind of cocoon in which to think, and even through my exhaustion, I felt the benefit of it. For a little while, my thoughts were a little less muddled.

What did I know to be an absolute truth? Very little, when it came right down to it. One of the only actual facts was that I had taken possession of a jewel that was rare and storied.

The other fact was that I'd heard Paul's voice on that answering machine. Luca wanted Paul to know I was involved, and by kissing me in front of the paparazzi had made sure of it. "How did you switch the bags?" I asked.

"You were sleeping. It was easy."

"But how did you know what bag I had? It was exactly the same as mine."

He looked at me. "I broke into your apartment in San Francisco."

"Why not just plant the jewel there?"

He paused. "If you came to Scotland, I knew you would be more likely to help me."

True enough. I *was* helping him, wasn't I? "So you spied on me? Broke into my home?"

"I did not touch anything. Except your cat. He's very nice." He gave me a half smile. "And, the purple underthings were very pretty, hanging on the shower."

"Don't be sly. That's disgusting."

"Expedient," he said, and leaned his head back on the seat. "That is all."

I grunted, and thought of my apartment, overlooking the beach in San Francisco. I paid a bloody fortune for it—and on my modest salary, I'd never have been able to afford it. It was the one thing I'd let my father do for me. Too far from the sea, and I began to feel restless and out of sorts.

"You should be better protected," he said. "The paintings are valuable, no?"

"Some of them." The collection of artwork on my walls was my prize possession and included a tiny sketch by Gaugin, purchased at God only knows what price by Paul for my seventeenth birthday. "Did you steal any of them?"

"No," he said. "I am jewel thief, and I wanted only to discover what model suitcase you owned." His voice was wearing down. "You need better security. It was very simple to break in."

I nodded. Luca fell silent. I thought of the Gaugin, of a collection of works done by a Tahitian painter from the modern world.

Which led to thoughts of Paul. In the darkness, with so much that involved him, it was impossible not to let the past swirl into my brain.

I don't even remember the first time I met him. I must have been five or six—he's part of that stretch of my parents' lives—and a race broke him when he was thirty-three, so it was before then.

It is said that I turned to my mother and said, "I am going to marry that man." She laughed when she told the story, and it used to embarrass me.

I don't remember our meeting, but I have hundreds of other memories of him over the years. He runs like a thread through everything.

He was a sort of artistic guardian, seeing to my education of the world—painters and literature and poets; how to eat and dine and serve; how to converse and be sparkling. We loved museums and saw them all eventually. He loved to take me to the seashore, too, and help me build sandcastles, buy me ices in Italy, ice cream in America. He was boyish and exuberant, unlike the other adults in my world.

I adored him. He had a long, angled face, with large gray-green eyes that could twinkle so beautifully, and big gentle hands.

So much of my childhood is woven through with Paul: bringing a bauble from some exotic jaunt; laughing down at me as I danced on his feet. He read me stories in his lilting, French-accented voice. Taught me to cook hardboiled eggs and serve them in egg cups—which he then collected for me from all over the world.

I know now that—

Never mind. My mother eventually made peace with him. She never truly loved any of my brash American father's racing friends, but Paul had a way about him that pierced even my mother's hard veneer. Like my grandmother, Paul was French, and that held some weight with both of them.

When I was ten, he slammed into a seawall at Monaco, totaling his car and landing in the hospital for nearly seven months. He broke two dozen bones, including his skull and his jaw, most of his ribs, and all the bones in his right arm and hand.

Everyone thought he would die. They were careful to warn me—he's gravely injured, they said. *It will be a miracle if he survives.*

I insisted that he would not die. Every day, I walked to the little Catholic church around the corner from our coral-painted house in Nice—my mother, being raised by her French mother, was that rarest of beings, a Scottish Catholic—and lit a candle for him. Every single day, I knelt before Mary, in her clean blue robes, and promised I would be good if Paul could just stay alive.

I begged to be allowed to see him, but they would not let me, not for weeks and weeks, during which he lay in a coma, unsupported by machines, but not conscious or aware. I fretted and complained and whined. Once, I tried to sneak in on my own.

At last, my grandmother, visiting our home in Nice from Scotland, took mercy on me. Brooking no argument from my parents, she drove me to the hospital where I could see for myself that Paul was still alive. Barely, but he could breathe on his own.

It scared me, of course—the tubes stuck into his skin and the plaster encasing his legs and arms and shoulders and head. His unmoving stillness seemed like the grave, but I put my hand on his and it was warm. It twitched, just the smallest bit.

Fiercely I said to him, "You must not die, Paul. I am here, waiting for you to wake up."

It was still another month before his coma dissolved, but I was there most days, waiting, talking, reading him stories from a collection of French fairy tales, which were not at all the sanitized, brushed-up American versions. I loved the very terrible things that lurked in French editions—they comforted me in some way that the less dark tellings did not.

I took my dolls in, and left a stuffed cat on his bed, which the nurses found charming. I learned to knit like my grandmother, and tried to knit lace as I sat at his bedside, watching the sky through the windows.

Every morning, before school, I detoured into the tiny church and lit candles to the Virgin, and to Saint Bernard, patron saint of racers. It was not clear, exactly, that Bernard would be of help to an auto racer, or healing, but his was the statue I could find, so it was to him I offered my petition.

The afternoon Paul did awaken, I was there all by myself, holding his big, knobby-knuckled hand. It was a blustery day, wind slamming sheets of rain into the windows, and I was watching it, fretting, wondering if he would ever wake up.

His fingers slowly curled around mine, warm and

large, and I turned slowly, to see him looking at me. A sideways smile lifted his lips on the left. "My Sylvie," he said, and the words sounded raw in the voice that had not uttered a word in all that time.

I flung myself on him. "Paul!"

His other hand came up and touched the back of my head. "Sweet Sylvie. I heard you."

In my relief, I cried and cried. That day, I took flowers and all my accumulated little bits of money and offered them to the saints who had saved his life.

Offerings to saints had become a habit. I needed to make the offerings on my own behalf now.

# *Chapter 8*

Diamond, the hardest known material, is pure carbon, crystallized under a very high pressure and temperature. In nature, such an environment exists only at depths of 150 to 200 km below the surface of the earth. Volcanic eruptions drive the diamond-bearing rocks called "Kimberlite" and "Lamproite" to the surface of the earth where the diamonds can be extracted.
—www.costellos.com.au

The caravan park sat on a spit of level ground nearby the sea. By day, the views were spectacular—the sea and hills, a ruined castle, and in the distance, an unruined one. My preference was always for those that were not spit-shined and orderly; my mother had loved the gardens at Culzean, the topiary and paths and the gilt within the castle itself, and my great-grandmother often spoke of her childhood walking those lanes to Sunday school, she and her sisters, along the beach and up the long, long stairs to the castle.

But my taste was for the neglected ones. They didn't have to be falling down, but I wanted them to myself so I could hear their stories, put my hands on the walls and feel the past vibrating through the stones. I wanted the possibility—however thin—that I might find some forgotten relic, some dropped thing from a hundred or even a thousand years ago. It was the romantic in me.

Which was the part I'd been trying to kill now for at least a decade. My mother's life, then my own, had shown me there was no such thing as soul mates or eternal love, and intellectually, I'd given up believing in them.

Emotionally…well, that was more difficult. The heart wants to believe all kinds of things, doesn't it? And what was I doing in my work—specializing in legendary jewels. Hard to imagine anything more romantic than that. Being in Scotland made me remember…

The view from the caravan at night depended upon how many people were around, and how many lights were on, and what the weather was like.

Sometimes, a full moon could make the seascape and hills seem hauntingly cold and lonely. Tonight, there was no moon, only the cloud-washed sky, faintly gray, and the sea spray in the air. I saw no other lights in the caravans. It was a place for week-enders, summer getaways. At midweek in late March, there was no one about at all. I found the key beneath the flower pot, and let myself in; Luca came in behind me.

It was very cold inside, but the light went on when I flicked the switch. It was ordinary and tidy, the big front window facing the darkness of the water, a table with bench seats tucked beneath it. In the back were two bedrooms and a shower.

As I leaned against the counter, I suddenly felt again the slam of jet lag. I *really* needed some sleep. The lack of it made my neck and shoulders feel as brittle and hard as an old book.

"Sit down," I told Luca. "I'll find the first-aid kit."

I turned on the stove, a space heater that would warm the area quickly, then shuffled through the cupboards in the small kitchen area. There was a first-aid kit in a drawer, and I took it out, along with a face cloth.

Only then did I look back to Luca. In the light, the blood looked gruesome, crusted in his hair and on his face, gumming up his eyebrow. His skin was pale, and the angle of the light made his cheeks look hollow, like a skeleton or death.

"Jeez," I said lightly, and turned on the water to let it warm up a little. "You probably needed stitches."

He lowered the hand that held the wad of tissues, and the cut over his brow leaked a little. "Scalp wound," he said with a shrug. "They bleed a lot, no?"

I carried the wet, warm rag to him and began to gently wash the blood that had dried on his face. A very good face it was, too, with tan skin stretched thinly over cheekbones, high brow, the strong bridge of his nose. His lashes were thick and inky, like his hair, the nose strong, lips full. Exotic. As intimacy goes, hand to face or head is very high, and I felt the thrill and recklessness of it as I tended him. He kept his eyes cast down. It helped.

Finally, I got to the cut, which was—despite his protests—deep enough it should have had stitches. The bleeding was slowing, but a small patch of gray bone showed. I blanched a little, but managed to get it clean, then bandaged with a sterile patch of white strapped into place with strips of white first-aid tape.

Only then did he raise his eyes. He took my hand, raised it to his lips and kissed the second and third knuckles, and looked up at me. "Thank you."

In the light, the blue irises were astonishing. Not a single fleck of gold or green or any other color, just shades of blue. Grade D for clarity.

"You're welcome," I said, taking my hand away. I

dropped the soiled rag into the sink. "Do you want a cup of tea?" I asked, filling the kettle.

"I'd prefer coffee, if there is any."

I chuckled, putting the kettle on the stove and lighting the burner beneath it. "Don't hold your breath." I opened the cupboard and took out a stainless steel kettle, big enough for several cups, and found the tea bags. There was sugar sealed in a plastic container, and powdered milk in a matching one. "Sorry, no coffee."

"There never is in the UK. I have *never* had a decent coffee here. Ever. It all tastes as if someone has put five grains of instant in the bottom of a cup and poured in three cups of water." He shuddered. "Awful."

"Right." I chuckled, and was rewarded with a quirk of smile. "May as well go for tea, then." As I waited for the water to come to a boil, I gathered up the scissors and tape and bandages and tucked them back into the kit. Individual packets of aspirin were nestled next to the iodine, and I pulled one out. "Headache?"

"It is unmanly to admit it," he said, but he held out his hand. I gave him the pills and a glass of water, then leaned on the counter as I waited for the kettle.

Again, I remembered the phone messages I hadn't heard and pulled out the phone to see if there was service here. The screen showed a little bear turning backward on the screen—success. "Finally," I said. "Isn't cell phone reception weird?"

I punched in the voice mail numbers, and wonder of wonders, it worked.

The service said, "You have three new messages," and I took the phone away from my ear to punch in the number to let me hear it. Luca stood, put his hand over mine.

"Wait," he said.

"What?"

"Check later," he said, and bent down to kiss me. He put the warmth of his palms exactly where I needed to feel them, flesh against those tight, tired muscles.

And it was just....so much simpler to be kissed, so pleasant to taste the richness of his mouth and breathe in that clove and orange scent—I half expected some cordial flavor to be on his tongue, like the syrup inside a chocolate bar.

I turned my head, angled my mouth to fit him better, and he made a soft noise, took a step closer, put his body against mine. His chest, his hips, our thighs touched. I felt his jeans on my bare knee. His hands slid from my shoulders to my hair, still damp in its braid. He just touched my scalp, shaped his palms to it, and moved his hips against me.

And there I stood, small of my back against the counter, cell phone forgotten in my hand, mouth open and drinking.

The kettle whistled. Luca slowly—reluctantly, it seemed to me—let me go. For an instant, he looked down at me, a soberness in his eyes I had not seen. Again I thought of the post-war industrialism of Bucharest, the grimness of an eastern European nation that had spent so much time struggling to hold its own.

*Stop it.*

He was a thief who'd stolen one of the most valuable diamonds in the world, double-crossed the man who'd no doubt paid him handsomely to steal it, then set me up to take the fall for him and carry the bloody—literally—gem across the continent to his homeland.

"How," I asked, snagging the screaming kettle, "did you get the jewel through security?"

He lifted one jet-black, glossy brow. "I say it is a bauble for my child."

I nodded. Because who would believe such a big stone was actually a real diamond?

"I'm going to find some warmer clothes," I said. "I'll be back in a minute."

In the bedroom, I pulled open drawers until I found some jeans. My cousin Alan wasn't a lot taller than I, and although they'd be baggy, they'd be a lot warmer than bare legs. As if to reinforce my decision, a gust of wind blew into the caravan walls. Rain came with it, falling in sideways sheets. I shivered and buttoned the jeans, then found a warm sweater to put on over the turquoise linen shirt I'd taken from Luca's bag.

Then, in the quiet of the bedroom, by myself, I took out the diamond and held it in my hand. She filled my palm, clear as water except that small, piercingly bright ruby floating within, like a heart or a bloody tear.

Again, I felt the depth of vibration within it, a magnetic tingling. All jewels—all rocks, actually—have a vibration, though I have been told not everyone can feel it. As far back as I can remember, however, my game was to walk along a beach or a path and keep my eyes open for intriguing stones. I'd then pick them up and clasp them in my hand to measure the vibrational hum they held. The strong ones I kept. The "cold" ones I left behind.

Gemstones nearly always have particularly strong vibrations. A gem is not only a rock but an object of desire, and they often have a history. They've absorbed the passions, the hungers, the sorrows and joys of those who have held them. I do not speak of this in scientific circles, of course. I'd be laughed out of the company of my peers, even if many of them could identify with me on some level.

But I do feel it, and I suspect so do many people. That's why we reach, instinctively, for ancient vases or put our hands flat on an old wall. Our need to feel everything is the reason for all those signs in museums that say Please do not touch!

The Katerina practically sizzled. I lifted her and pressed her to the brow chakra, between the eyebrows, the spot of the third eye. Sometimes, doing that, I feel a hum that's quite intense. Sometimes—I know it's crazy—there will be a picture, or maybe a color associated with it.

Crazy, no?

With the Katerina, I felt the buzzing sense of motion, energy against my forehead, and a sense of darkness. Not a surprise, considering the history of the stone. Luca was right—I didn't believe in curses, but I did know that stones seemed to absorb all kinds of emotion. Greed was a particularly destructive drive, and this stone was no doubt permeated with it.

My cell phone rang. I was concentrating so closely on the stone that I startled, and for the third time, I dropped the Katerina. It was as if the jewel was leaping out of my hands.

Where did she want to go? I wondered.

The phone rang again, and I grabbed it, flipped it open. "Hello?"

As I spoke, I bent down, snared the jewel, and slipped it back into the safe hiding spot of my bra.

"Sylvie?" said a voice on the other end of the line, as clear and near as if he was standing next to me.

I went still. "Paul?"

"Yes. Where are you? I tried your hotel. They said you were not there."

It's impossible to tell you how his voice affected me. How it always affected me. I've heard the word "dulcet" all my life, but Paul is the only man I've known who really had a voice that could be described that way—honeyed and melodious. It was the pitch of a cello, and his English was thickly, charmingly accented. In my mind's eye, I saw his face, long and harshly carved, his eyes a greenish-gray that that could, by turns, be stormy or cold or vividly fierce.

With some hostility, I asked, "How did you get this number?"

"I called your grandmother. Have you not received my messages?"

"No, I haven't been able to get—"

"Where are you?" he asked again.

"In Scotland."

Luca knocked at the bedroom door. He'd obviously heard the phone ring. "Sylvie?"

I looked over my shoulder at the door, frowning. In my ear, Paul said, "I know you're in *Scotland*. Where?"

"I don't know that that's any of your business," I said.

At the door, Luca knocked again, both polite and insistent. "Sylvie?

"Just a minute," I said in the direction of the door. "I'm not dressed."

Paul said, "Is there someone with you?"

"Again, none of your business," I said. Through the fabric of the sweater, my shirt, my bra, I rubbed the Katerina.

Paul said, "I have never lied to you, Sylvie. Would you agree?"

His voice. God, his voice. I bent my head, pressed the phone close to my ear. Because I knew him so well, I was sure that right now, he'd be sitting down, and he might be drawing circles on a piece of paper. Circles or ovals, or jagged, electric-looking patterns, depending on his mood. Sometimes, the circles took on faces—nose, eyes, hair, neck. Sometimes, the ovals became feet or fingernails on a hand.

"No, you've never lied to me," I said. "Not as far as I know."

"Good. Listen, *ma poulette*, do you have the jewel?"

"It *was* you, on the phone! That message in Paris!"

"Yes. I am currently away, but I picked up my voice mail this afternoon. What is going on, Sylvie?"

At the door, Luca knocked again. "Sylvie, are you all right?"

I went to the door, opened it, pretending there was nothing wrong. I nodded, pressed my finger to my lips. Mouthed, "Paul."

He looked grim.

On the phone, Paul said, "Sylvie, are you there?"

"Yes, and I'm fine," I said.

"Do you have the jewel?"

"You know the answer to that question."

"You do not have it by accident, *ma cherie*."

"No sh—" I stopped myself in time. He hated to hear me swear crudely. "Kidding."

"Please, Sylvie," he said. "Listen to me. You will meet a man named Luca Colceriu. Do not trust him."

"Already made his acquaintance," I said, and met Luca's gaze. There was something hot and black in his eyes, and a hair-thin line of white around his finely cut nostrils, betraying the strong emotion he was attempting to hide. "He's standing right here."

*"Merde!"* Paul said.

Luca scowled, shook his head, flung away his hands.

"He is very dangerous, Sylvie. Ruthless and ambitious." I raised an eyebrow and waited. If they'd wanted some silly little pawn to position and play, they should have chosen a different woman. Luca could be excused, but Paul could not.

Into the phone, I said quietly, "I can take care of myself, Paul."

"I have never doubted it."

"What do you want me to do?"

For a moment, silence roared between us. Quietly, he said, "Call me when you can."

"So you can warn me about another man I'm involved with?"

"Ah, sweet, you are still angry with me over Timothy."

My ex.

"No. Why would I be angry? You were right."

"And that is why you have not spoken to me in five years, because I was right?"

I ducked away from Luca's avidly listening ears. "No. I don't know. Maybe."

"Sylvie, *venez à moi dans l'Arran*," he said in French. *Come to me in Arran.*

Arran. Not in this lifetime.

"I'm taking the jewel to the inspector," I said, and hung up.

# Chapter 9

*Carat* is the 4th C. This is the size of the diamond. One carat is divided into 100 "points," so that a diamond of 75 points weighs .75 carats. Carat weight is the most obvious factor in determining the value of a diamond. But two diamonds of equal carat weights can have very unequal prices, depending on their quality, and diamonds of high quality can be found in all size ranges.

—www.costellos.com.au

The line went dead. I held the phone a moment longer, feeling a thread reeling out from my ear, across the miles and the years to Paul, to my grandmother, who would be worrying now that he'd talked to her.

Against my breast, I felt the living jewel humming with power.

Luca said, "You must not believe what he says about me, Sylvie. He is very angry with me."

"I've known him a lot longer than I've known you."

"And he is like a father to you, no?"

Stung as always by this spin, I lifted a shoulder. "No." But I remembered again that I wanted to talk to my father. What time was it in Kuala Lampur? I punched the button for the World Clock option on my phone and looked at the little red dot traveling around the globe. "Where is Malaysia, exactly?" I asked.

"In Asia somewhere." Luca scowled. "I don't know."

The map didn't give me many choices. "Closer to Thailand or Singapore?" I frowned. "I think it's south of Thailand."

"That sounds correct, yes."

Only five thirty there. Too early. I clipped the phone closed.

"Paul is protective of you. He's also furious with me." Luca smiled, ruefully. "You know him—would he have anything good to say of my character at such a time?"

"No."

He spread his hands, as if to say, *you see?*

I thought of the police, who would be expecting

me in a few days, and what they would think of my consort, the jewel thief. Even the very fact that I'd had the jewel now for some six hours without notifying them spoke rather loudly, didn't it?

I did not look away from Luca's brilliant gaze. "What do you want with this jewel?"

"Only to return it to Romania," he said.

"Nothing else?"

"Nothing," he said, and raised his hands, palm up. "I swear."

I tucked the phone into my front pocket, rubbed the obviously comatose third eye between my brows. "Let's have our tea."

"Yes."

We returned to the kitchen area, and settled at the table before the wide window, now obscured by waves of sideways rain. "It's turned into a bad night," I said, pouring steaming tea from the stainless steel pot.

"It will make it more difficult for anyone to follow us."

"No one followed us. I would have seen them."

"Would you?" He stirred four spoonfuls of sugar into his mug of tea.

I raised an eyebrow.

He shrugged. "It's my weakness."

In answer to his question, I said, "I would know if someone followed us, yes. On those dark little roads?"

"Someone must have followed you earlier, or else how did that man in your room know you were there?"

I narrowed my eyes, thought about it. "I don't know. It would be easier to follow me from the airport."

"But who knew you had the jewel?"

"Aside from you, you mean?"

He nodded.

"I made a phone call."

"To?"

I shook my head. "None of your business." But would Paul have sent a man to steal the jewel from me?

No. There were many possibilities, but that wasn't one of them.

"Do not be too trusting, *prieten,*" Luca said.

I glared at him. "Don't be a cliché." A hard gust of wind slammed into the caravan, making it rock slightly, and I shivered. "What do you know? What about others, criminals, who might want the jewel for themselves? Who knew about it?" I gave him a hard look. "If you want me to trust you, tell me what's going on."

"I am not certain I know everything."

"Why did he hire you?"

"To steal it."

I frowned. "That doesn't really make sense to me, Luca. I mean, just out of the blue, he hired you to steal one of the most famous diamonds in the world?"

"More or less, yes."

"It's been missing for decades. Where did Gunnarsson get it? Where was it all this time?"

"That, I do not know."

I absorbed that for a moment. Then, "Who killed him, then? And why didn't they take the other jewels?"

His eyelids dropped, and again I had that sense of shuddering that came from him. It must have been a terrible scene. "The police think it was an enemy, another drug runner," he said. "Isn't that right?"

"Yes."

"It was more crude than that. Gunnarsson was a very wealthy man, and he liked collecting beautiful things, as your Paul does."

"So?"

"His apartment was filled with many things that could have been stolen—he liked sculpture, art glass and objets d'art. There were those eggs, you know— Faberagé."

"What about them?"

"Some with diamonds and things, you know?" His mouth worked. "None of them were stolen, either."

"How do you know?"

His elegantly beautiful hands—the hands of a musician, or a lover, or a…thief—spread open around the cup. "I heard."

"Heard?"

"A friend of a friend."

Tension made my neck tight. "You're lying. And

I'm not going to play if you lie. Get it? You want me
to carry this freaking diamond, tell me the truth."

He pursed his lips. "All right," he said, and looked
at me. There was new steeliness there. "You will not
like it. Your Paul—" he emphasized and drew out the
name "—will not look so sweet to you at the end of
this telling."

"I have no illusions about Paul Maigny," I said.

"Don't you?" He inclined his head, those blue eyes
sharpening on my face. "Do you know that your eyes
grow warm when you speak of him?"

"What I know," I said, "is that he is a collector, that
his childhood taught him to be shrewd, that he's quite
determined when he sets his mind to a thing."

"He will stop at nothing to have what he wants."

"That's probably exaggerating."

"I don't think so," Luca said, meeting my eyes.
"Here is the story—Paul was in negotiations with an
art dealer for the Katerina, bidding against another
collector for it. Unfortunately, the dealer had a little
problem with drugs and gambling, and ran afoul of
his supplier—"

"Gunnarsson, I assume?"

"Yes. Gunnarsson was going to cut him off.
Because he was so desperate, the art dealer gave up
the Katerina, which The Swede very much wanted
because it was Maigny—your Paul—who wanted it.

"When he hired me to steal the jewel back, he paid

me half upfront. The rest of the payment were to be the jewels in the collection."

"*All* of them? Jeez."

"All of them together were not worth a fraction of the Katerina, of course, but for me, it would be a simple matter to find collectors and dealers who would make me quite rich. I could not, on my own, find a buyer for a jewel so expensive as the Katerina."

"I see. And Maigny only wanted the Katerina to *have* it, not to sell it."

"Yes."

He sipped his tea, his eyes on the dark window, the slams of rain. "I am no ordinary thief," he said, and looked at me. "I am very, very good at what I do. In some circles, I'm—" he gave me a wry little smile that managed to be self-deprecating and deliciously seductive all at once "—quite renowned."

"That doesn't surprise me."

"For a month, I planned every detail. Had it worked, it would have been the last job I had to do."

I nodded, filing the information away. "So what went wrong?"

"I arrived as anticipated, while Gunnarsson was out. The Katerina was in a safe by itself, and I'd secured it, and was working on cracking the other safe when—" He winced, shook his head. "He returned. Too early. And there was something wrong—he was afraid, plainly. I hid, and then three men came in, garroted him, and were obviously going to come after the Katerina, so I bolted. Out the back and into the night." He laced his fingers together, touched the tips of his thumbs, point to point. "I'd planned well, so I was able to get away. I hid out in a room nearby the train station that night, trying to decide what to do. In the morning, it was reported that the police had found him dead, and seized his jewels."

A chill rippled down my spine. "So who were the men? Why didn't they steal his jewels?"

"They might not have known about them. They think it was a drug killing."

I searched my memory for details. "I don't remember a lot about the actual murder. It didn't particularly interest me at the time." But I frowned. "It all seems too convenient. You just happened to be stealing the Katerina when these guys come in and murder him and they don't even know that he collects all these jewels?"

He shrugged, and my gut said it was genuine bewilderment on his face. "I don't know. They said it was Peruvians, that he'd crossed someone."

I narrowed my eyes. "The man in my room wasn't Peruvian."

"No, I don't think so."

"Hmm." It seemed there was some answer right in front of my eyes, but I couldn't quite capture it. "I don't think it was Paul who killed Gunnarsson, either."

"Maybe it was the police?"

"That's reaching," I said dismissively.

"And when the murders happened, you were cheated of your payoff and decided to keep the Katerina?"

Luca shook his head. "No. Until I held it, I did not intend to take it back to my country."

I looked at him.

"Stupid, hmm?" he said. "But once I saw her, it was as if I had no choice. I took her back to my hotel, and I waited there, trying to think what to do. And then of course the news hit the papers, and your name was raised, and I knew of your connection to Maigny— and *one thing led to another.*"

"And here we are."

"Yes."

We sat in the kitchen with our tea, each to our own thoughts. The tea was soothing, hot, sweet. In the silence between bursts of wind, I heard the overhead light buzzing faintly.

"Enough of all that." Luca smiled, his healthy white teeth flashing. "My grandmother is a gypsy," he said. "Shall I read your palm?"

I rolled my eyes. "Let me guess," I said. "I'm going to meet someone tall, dark and handsome."

He raised an eyebrow, his eyes twinkling. "That has already happened." With a sideways smile, he bent over my palm and spread open my fingers. It seemed somehow intensely intimate, previewing a different sort of spreading, and I found heat touching my ears, a strange, Victorianesque reaction.

He brushed the hollow and pads and rises with the very tips of his fingers, and in my weariness, I was mesmerized by the look of his fingernails, clean half moons, somehow sturdy-looking.

"Mmmm," he said, and traced a line down the middle of my hand, top to bottom. "This is a fame line," he said. "Not everyone has one. It means you will attain great reputation through your work."

"Or I'll be a pet of the paparazzi."

He flashed a quick smile. "Here the heart and life line join. You are stubborn, but felt betrayed by your family."

"I'm so not amazed that you knew that."

He went back to the perusal of my palm, and he seemed absurdly serious after a few minutes, studying this and that, lifting my hand to see more light on the palm, grunting a little.

"Will you stop that? You're scaring me."

"You have markings that are most unusual. Having one is interesting, two would be a surprise. I have not seen anyone with three." He looked up at me. "You have a very powerful destiny, Sylvie."

"Again, that's my father's mark in my life. He's the famous one."

"You will be, too, for work you do yourself. A fame line comes from your own efforts." He made an *x* on the pad below my forefinger. "This is a star of destiny. It's very powerful, this mark. It's the one that says you will experience greatness in some endeavor."

I gave him a half smile. "You sound so serious."

His glossy lashes did not lift. "I have never seen these marks, Sylvie, though I have heard people speak of them. It is intriguing." Again he stroked the lines. "I wonder what it is you will do?"

I didn't want destiny or anything difficult for tonight, and said, noncommitally, "Who knows?" I took a breath. "Tell me something else."

"This," he said, moving his finger, "is your heart line. It is both strong and broken at times. You will love boldly, and your heart will break. It has broken twice to now."

I must have winced or jerked, because he looked at me in surprise. "Yes? Twice?"

"Well, how hard would that be to guess? I'm old enough to have had at least two."

He pointed to the middle line, side to side. "And there is marriage here, though I do not see children." A frown pulled his brows toward that aggressive nose. He tipped my hand to the side, looking at the edge. "Ah, here. Perhaps one child after all. That's good."

"I'm not sure I'm all that interested."

"No," he said, without looking at me, "you are a woman who will find pleasure in your child. A daughter, perhaps," he added, raising his eyes, "to spoil a little, no?"

I shrugged lightly, but I liked the idea of it, somewhere deep inside of me. A daughter, yes. With my mother's thin nose and graceful hands.

Keeping his eyes on my face, he lifted my hand to his lips. I didn't pull away—I let him press my knuckles, one at a time to the heat of his lush mouth. Just beyond the angle of my knuckle was a hint of moisture, the give of flesh.

One kiss, two, three…

I was exhausted, disoriented by the shift in circumstances, and much too drawn to him. I took my hand away. "Let's not," I said.

"Are you afraid of me?"

"It would be the sensible thing," I answered, "but no."

That pleased him. His white teeth showed. "Good."

As I sat there, the world started to drag, like an old-fashioned cartoon, the sound slowing and slowing, even while I peered at him, genuinely trying to concentrate. Jet lag was starting to press into the folds of my brain like a hot towel, pressing down, ever thicker, into the creases of gray matter until all systems were buzzing with exhaustion.

"I have to sleep," I said abruptly, standing, not even caring if it seemed rude.

Automatically, I checked the locks on the doors, tugged the curtains over the stove closed, put spoons and cups into the sink. "Help yourself to whatever you need," I said. "You can sleep in the second room, just there." I pointed out the door.

"Thank you," he said, standing. The bandage stood out in a white rectangle on his tanned forehead. A curl stuck to it, glossy black. He seemed shy as he said, "May I sleep with you? Not for sex, just to lie down with a human on such a cold night?"

"Do women really fall for that line?" I said, blinking irritably.

"Sylvie—" he said, reproach in his voice.

I shook my head. My braid swung with the movement. "I don't care what you do. Stay. Go. Whatever you want. I'm to bed."

He followed me into the room, and we crawled under the big thick coverlet, soft flannel stuffed with batting. No top sheet, just that muffling weight of cover boring down on my body. I fluffed my pillows, put one between us.

God. It felt wonderful to just stop moving, to lie down instead of sitting upright. "I am so tired!"

Luca murmured. His body warmth was like a hot water bottle, taking the chill off the bed. Near the ball of my right foot was the arch of his left. I would have to be careful not to curl up around him.

He settled his hand on my hip. "Is this all right?"

"Yeah."

I sighed into the softness of the bed. Wind buffeted

the caravan, almost rocking it with gusts, and the sound of the driving rain muffled even the sound of the surf not far away on the rocks.

Somehow, the combination made me think sleepily of Paul. Because I was so tired, my usual defenses were gone, and memories flooded into my half-sleeping brain.

I thought of a Frenchman with long, elegant hands.

To distract myself I said to Luca, "If you are descended from royalty, does that mean you are royal yourself?"

"Minor."

"You are minor royalty?"

"Cousins to the royal family. Not that there has been a monarch for a long time, so it doesn't matter."

"So why did you become a thief? You seem intelligent. Why crime?"

"My father," Luca said, "was a hero. He fought the communists in my country, and he was killed. My mother, her heart was broken, and she did not last long afterward."

He paused so long that I dozed, waiting for the answer. "I became a thief to prove you have to take what you want. To prove myself," he said, his voice growing softer. "Now I would like to show that I am more the man my father was."

Fathers. Noble, or not. Honorable, or not. Available,

or not. Mothers get so much of the credit and blame in our lives, but fathers leave indelible marks, too.

I thought of my own father, and of others who had wanted to prove themselves. All my unresolved issues, which had been stirred up and lurking all day, came pouring out of the box where they mainly lived under lock and key—parent issues, mostly. The usual things a girl gets snared in when her mother dies too young.

I thought, unavoidably now, of Paul.

I was twelve. A vulnerable age in a lot of ways, and a moment ripe for planting all sorts of things, and I have the usual abandonment issues that go along with sudden death.

And it was very sudden. I know now that she and my father were on the verge of divorce because of my father's perpetual infidelities, that she was back in Scotland trying to find a place for us to live when she was killed in a most prosaic car accident: a woman in a hurry to get home from work ran a stop sign, and broadsided my mother's car. My mother's head was banged just right and she died. No flames, no big spinout. Just a stupid, pointless death.

I don't remember my father being at the funeral. Intellectually, I know he was there, but I can't see him in my imagination. It was Paul holding my hand when she was buried, Paul who held me later as I sobbed and sobbed that afternoon, growing more and more hysterical until he picked me up, carried me to the bathroom of my grandmother's house and washed my face with cold water. He forced a brandy down my throat.

When I'd finally fallen asleep, he talked my father into letting him take me away for a holiday for a few weeks, just until the worst of the shock wore off. Somewhere warm, where the sun could bake away some of my slashing pain.

My grandmother—that would be Sylvie, the Frenchwoman I'm named for—adored Paul, and from that summer in Nice, knew we had a special bond. My father was absent that year, racing or drinking or otherwise trying to kill himself. I sometimes wonder if he remembers any of it.

We went to Tahiti, Paul and I, ostensibly so that he could teach me about the great painters who'd done their work in that land, the French Gauguin, first, of course, but also van Gogh. He booked a cabana on a beach, where we heard the turquoise waters swishing up on the white beaches. Wind rustled the pine trees. It was so far away. So exotic.

We swam. We studied painters—Gauguin and van Gogh, Matisse and Boullaire. We explored writers, too—Robert Louis Stevenson, a restless Scot, and Jack London, whom I liked, and Melville, who bored me. He read aloud from the journals of Pierre Loti, and I liked that, too.

Paul coaxed me to eat with papayas and mangos and delicate monkfish. He bought me rosary beads made of polished coral, to remind me that I'd always have a mother. At night, he stayed up late long after I went to bed, drinking. I don't know if he loved her as a woman, or merely as a friend, but his grief was true and deep.

There is a photo from that trip that still sits on my mantle. Paul is tall and tan, his beard grown out a few days worth on his chin. His hair is longish, lionlike. He looks thin to me, his hands too big for his wrists, his cheeks gaunt. I am leaning on his shoulder, my head sideways so my crown is against his neck. We both look haunted.

And yet, at the end of a few weeks, we returned to Nice, where my father was living. Paul went back to Paris.

And things were all right for a while. Then my father moved us to Brazil.

# *Chapter 10*

The next most important element of the 4 C's of diamond grading is *color*. Color is classified by letters, ranging from "D," colorless, to "Z," yellow. The final category of color rating is "fancy", such as red, pink, blue, and strong yellow. Many are highly prized. One famous example is the vivid blue Hope Diamond.

—www.costellos.com.au

Back in the present, in the darkness of my cousin's caravan, I startled as my sleep foot took a dream step into a void. For a moment, I lay there blinking, confused over my location, the strong smell of oranges in the room, the unfamiliar—

I looked at the man attached to the hand on my hip. Oh. Yes.

I glanced at the digital clock. We'd only been lying here maybe an hour, if that. What had startled me into wakefulness? I stared into the dark, listening, but heard only the whipping, roaring wind and rain. It must have been—

Car doors slammed. Next to me, Luca bolted upright. He pressed fingers to my lips before leaping up to peer out the window. He swung back and bent down close to whisper, "There is someone out there."

I shifted, tried to find the comfortable hollow in the bed that I'd been so enjoying a moment ago. "I'm sure it's just a neighbor. Let's sleep."

"I do not think your neighbors are carrying baseball bats, no?"

"What?" I stood up to look out the window. Rain was pouring down still, the darkness nearly absolute except for the pool of light that glowed from the caravan itself, not so much light under most circumstances, but more than enough on such a dark night to show me a small car and the three men headed our way. "Who are they? How did they find us?"

"I do not know."

I dived for my shoes, jamming my feet into them hard. "What do we do?" My mind was full of images of a drug lord garroted, his throat spilling blood down his white shirt front.

Luca turned, putting his hands on my upper arms. "Listen, Sylvie, get out of here, go back to Ayr. I'll find you."

I yanked free. "Stop with the *Last of the Mohicans* crap, all right?" From the hook where I'd left it, I grabbed my coat, and without thinking, put my hand over the knot in my bra, reassuring myself that the Katerina was still there beneath my left breast.

Luca saw the gesture and smiled bitterly. "Do not let it seduce you, love."

I shoved my hands into my coat sleeves. "Don't worry. I can handle it. I'm not going to go to Ayr. I have too much family there."

"You must get away. Now. As fast as you can."

"Where, then, do you want to meet?"

I cast around in my mind. "Troon," I said. I had a cousin who'd been working the hospitality industry there. It was renowned for its golf, and boasted a famous old pub. "The Ship's Inn."

"I'll—"

There was a racket at the front door. "I'll try to come behind you," Luca said, and with a cry, he slammed his elbow into the glass of the window. It was strong, tempered or something, and didn't break. "Go!" he cried.

"Where?" I cried. "That's the only door."

From the front of the caravan came a slamming sound—maybe the door giving way. I thought fleetingly that my cousin Alan was going to kill me, but then Luca was slamming his elbow into the glass of the bedroom window.

One—slam! Two, slam! Three, slam, slam!

He swore. "It won't break!'

I looked around for something heavy. In the front of the caravan was a crashing sound. I thought I could feel the whole building rock, as if they'd bashed it sideways. They weren't in yet, anyway—they were no more successful than we were at breaking the slatted glass. That was something.

The room was tidy as a pin, but there was a trophy of some kind on the dresser. A big fish was on top—fishing trophies? Who knew?—but the base was a very heavy lead-feeling thing.

From the front room came a very loud crash and the sound of voices. The baseball bat had obviously done the trick.

I grabbed the trophy. "Get out of the way!"

Luca ducked. I swung the trophy as hard as I could into the window. It gave way with a somehow sibilant tinkling of safety glass, and the night came rushing in—soaking wet and cold.

"Let's get out!" I said in a low, urgent voice, and turned back to the door, trying to think of ways to get through that bedroom door to the kitchen where my purse—and thus, my keys—was.

Luca must have made it through the window, because I felt a gust of rain slap the back of my head as the door to the bedroom burst open. Without letting the intruder have a chance, or even getting much of a look at him, I barreled forward, swinging the trophy. It caught him squarely across the nose, the fish fins doing an admirable job of slashing his skin.

He slammed backward with a roar, and even in the dark, I saw the line of blood spring open across his face. I didn't wait to see if he'd recover, but slammed him again a second time, and turned around to climb out the window.

With a roar, he grabbed for me, catching my coat as I tried to dive out the window. He was a big guy, all right, and it didn't take a lot for him to yank me upward, clear off my feet.

It took even less for him to toss me toward the wall. My shoulder slammed into the dresser and I nearly dropped the trophy. I managed to shift sideways soon enough to avoid smashing my entire face into the drawers.

I knew how to fight, thanks to a stint in a truly dangerous school in Rio when I was fifteen, where "gangs" took on an entirely new meaning. My father was at the worst of his decline that year, blaming himself for my mother's death, drinking and carousing and generally attempting self-destruction. It was very nearly successful. When he finally emerged from his insanity, he had to spend two weeks in the hospital, recovering from "exhaustion."

It very nearly killed me, as well. The neighborhood required more than a girl of fourteen is generally required to deliver. Luckily, I wasn't a quitter, and I'd at least had the advantage of living in many places, fitting into many cultures. This one was closed, but I learned enough to get by.

Tonight, I had cause to be thankful for the lessons in street fighting.

It had been a very long time, but there are things you never forget. As soon as my feet touched the floor, I curled my body and then sprang upward as he tried to grab me, and swung back with the trophy, aiming for his knee. It connected with a sound like a knife into a chicken—*thunk*. The man made a strangled, choking cry, and I dived for the door, pushing away from him, scrambling across the floor to get away.

With a cry, he grabbed my hair and one ankle, his enormous hand like a vise around the bones. He yanked, and I went down, flat on my belly. My chin hit the floor, slamming my teeth together. The Katerina jammed upward into my breast so hard I got tears in my eyes, but there wasn't time for weakness.

With a growl, I used the leverage of his foot on my ankle to swing around, and brought the trophy down on his head. I felt the impact through my whole arm, and this time, he collapsed.

I didn't wait to see if it lasted—I scrambled for the door, bringing my trophy weapon with me. An absurd little voice, as if it were a commercial for trophy-as-weapon, said, "It's two weapons in one—club and knife."

What more does a girl need?

At the door, I had the great good fortune to meet contestant number two, coming to the aid of his compatriot. In a flash of light from somewhere beyond—headlights?—I saw his balding head and grim, piggy eyes. I recognized the man from the rental counter at the airport. Some instinct made me head backward. He was a giant, one of those hulking, neckless guys who do very well in American football.

I had to think fast. When those girl gangs would narrow in on you, it would usually be three girls, and they'd trap you in a little alley or narrow spot where they could kick your ass without anyone seeing. The only way to survive was to either run away, or fight back as long as they were kicking you practically to death. If you submitted to the beating, they'd kill you.

That was the choice here. Even with the heavy weapon, I couldn't bring this guy down. The girl gangs usually stopped short of death, but I didn't think this guy would mind much if he left a dead body or two behind.

That left the dash.

One good thing about fighting guys versus fighting girls, though—you can always get a man to double over for a second. I scrambled backward to the bed, as if I were afraid, and when he came toward me, I swung that trophy at his trophy for all I was worth.

Bull's-eye.

He dropped and I made a break for it, dashing around him and down the hall.

Rain was pouring in the caravan through the open front door, blown by the gusts of wind onto the linoleum. Damn, Alan would be so mad at me!

Running, I grabbed my purse off the counter and looped the long strap over my head, so the bag was nestled close to my waist, securely fastened to leave my arms and hands free. Hearing someone come behind me, I didn't bother with anything else, and dashed out into the blinding rain.

My feet landed in a puddle of sucking mud, nearly taking me down. I righted my balance, yanked my right foot out of the muck, and tried to get my bearings.

There's rain, and then there's Scottish rain. This was blinding, sideways, driving rain, the misery of which one must experience at least once. I literally could not see at thing, and for a minute, couldn't even figure out where the car was parked.

I heard men, grunting, fighting nearby, perhaps.

Someone shouted in a heavy Scottish accent, "Get her! She's got the fucking jewel!"

I had a second to wonder how they knew, when Luca shouted, "Sylvie, go!"

"Luca?"

"Go!"

His voice was thin, nearby, but when I whirled around, I couldn't see him at all. "Where are you?"

Then the wind took a breath, the rain started falling downward instead of sideways, and I spied the car, perfectly illuminated just long enough for me to put my head down and dash toward it, dash being hyperbole here, since my feet were squishing, sticking, slipping in the mud. I was soaked to the skin, but the rain offered as much protection for hiding me as it threw blocks in my way.

I got to the Spider, water pouring down the back of my neck, down my spine, icy cold. I scrambled for my keys, got them out and managed to get the door unlocked. Offering an apology to the car gods, I threw myself into the seats, knowing the wet would ruin the gorgeous interior. I reached behind me to close the door—

And was knocked sideways by a hammy fist with plenty of bone inside of it. The punch landed on the side of my head, and my keys went flying into the interior of the car somewhere. It felt like my head was slammed nearly off my body. Stars sparked on the edges of my right eye. For a second, I was blinking, stunned.

A gust of rain slammed into my face, driving salt water up my nose. I choked, started coughing. It shook the daze off my brain, and when the goon's hand closed around my upper arm, I was ready, shoving the sharp end of my elbow into his gut, then kicking with a backward, inexpert dodge. He shoved himself between me and the door, yanking with his Frankenstein-sized fist while I wrapped one arm around the steering column and held on. With my right elbow, I slammed backward as hard as I could. It was impossible to get leverage, and I growled in frustration. "Let me go!"

"C'mon, gerl," he said, "just let me have it and we'll be done w'ye."

I put my foot against the inside of the car and flung myself backward, hoping to break his grip. He slapped me, hard, and I tasted blood inside my mouth.

"Bastard!" With a growl, I bent over and bit down on his hand with all my might. He cried out and let go, and I shoved him backward, closed the door, and locked it. He slammed his fist into the window, and it cracked a little but didn't break. I yelped, and found myself ducking in case he punched all the way through. If anyone could, he'd be a good candidate.

He kicked the door, slammed a fist on the roof. Scrambling on the floor in the dark, my breath panting out of me in moist heat, fogging up the windows, I finally found the key on the floor of the passenger side.

Frankenstein slammed his fist into the window again, and I knew if he got to the windshield, I'd be in big trouble. Even if he didn't break it, he could easily damage it so badly I wouldn't be able to see out. With shaking hands, I got the key in the ignition and started the car. The engine caught with a roar. The sound steadied me, the feel of the wheel, the seat, the machine all around me. I flung the car into Reverse, away from him, took one second to fasten the seat belt, then slammed the car into gear and headed up the narrow spit of gravel to the main road.

Such as it was—a narrow ribbon of pavement circling the edge of the hills, with cliffs on the left, plunging down the rocks to ocean below, the fields and hills to the right, black and unfathomable in the darkness. It wound and looped up the west coast, this road, climbing and descending in ways that could be dizzying under the best of circumstances.

And these were hardly ideal circumstances. Even I was intimidated. The rain came over the car in waves, as if the ocean itself had become airborne. It was only a little better than being out on my own feet, because at least the windshield had wipers to give me a glimpse now and then of the road, and the headlights pierced the grim weather a hint.

I headed north, with the eventual goal of Troon, not far north of Ayr. A part of me knew I was headed for Androssan, though I had no hope I'd get that far on such a grim night. It was about ten kilometers or so to Alloway and then Ayr, with a string of villages that would give some light, anyway. If I could get that far, maybe to a small stretch of area that had a few lights and population, maybe I could wait out the rest of the storm.

No one appeared to be behind me. It was only the dark and the rain and me in the car, alone in the gruesome weather. Wind buffeted the little vehicle. I smelled the ocean, sharp and strong. I straightened in my seat, shook off the cold as the heater started to pump out warm air, and settled myself in to drive seriously.

I turned on the radio, without much hope of a signal, but a mournful Celtic tune came out of the speakers. It was company of a sort. Maybe we'd get some upbeat drums or fiddles after a time, rather than just grim tales of disaster and despair and love gone wrong.

What was it about Gaelic folk songs, anyway? I let my mind turn it over—something to think about besides the very real possibility of plunging over a cliff to my death in an Alpha Romeo with a priceless jewel tucked in my bra. I thought of the quote from Yeats: "Being Irish, he had an abiding sense of tragedy, which sustained him through temporary periods of joy." Certainly seemed to hold true of

Scots, as well. All that drama and tragedy sung in the old songs.

A gust of wind caught the car and I swerved to correct. Tires hit the wet road just right, and the wind caught the tail of the car, and I was suddenly whipping around in a circle on the narrow, cliffside road, the car completely out of control.

## Chapter 11

Diamonds were also used as a poison. The stones were ground to a powder and put into the enemy's food and drink. Many prominent people's deaths were attributed to diamond poisoning.

—Margaret Odrowaz-Sypniewski, B.F.A.

It happened so fast, I hardly had time to do the usual inward screech—*ay yi yi yi yi!*—before instinct kicked in.

*Never lose your head*, my father's voice said. Steel nerves, they said of him, and the sound of his voice in my mind steadied me. He used to take me to safe places where he'd lead me to deliberately losing control of the car, so I would learn how it felt, and would know, in the very cells of my body, how to regain control.

Letting go of my high, taut nerves, I fell into the feeling of the car itself, the sensation of the frame around me, the tires on the road, the engine humming through the machinery of the car. My hands and arms, my feet and legs, my eyes, my body, became an extension of the vehicle. I downshifted and steered into the spin, bringing it down from the dizzying height of the punishing, whipping turns. As long as I didn't go over the edge, everything should be okay.

The car slammed into the hillside, hard enough to jolt my teeth, but it was finally enough to stop the spin. I let go of my breath, listened to the sound of the car around me. For a minute, I paused, feeling the heat of fear leak out of my lungs, the cold clamminess of certain death ease away from my forehead.

Inexplicably, I thought of my cat, Michael. A gigantic, silvery, fluffy Siamese mix, he was the opposite of the aloof and complaining cat of legend. He loved me, followed me from room to room. Sulked when I took out my suitcase to go away somewhere. I'd left him with my best friend, Janine, and I was sure she was taking good care of him, but it hurt me to imagine how he'd feel if something happened to me.

It made me furious, suddenly. How had I ended up

in this mess, with Frankenstein's thugs on my tail on a very bad night in the west of Scotland?

The answer, as it so often was, couldn't be blamed on anything but me running away from my life. Running from San Francisco and my ex-husband, who was quickly marrying someone else, before even a full year had elapsed. Marrying money, which is what he'd thought he was doing with me. A fair assumption, since my father is so rich. And it's not like I'm poor or even struggling, but my father spends a lot, spends fast and furiously and I'm not likely to have much of an inheritance unless he dies early before he has a chance to spend it all. And only then if the wife-of-the-moment doesn't have some great team of lawyers.

It's always humiliating to lose out to another woman, but there's nothing quite like realizing you were being used. Paul tried to tell me, too, which is why I still haven't spoken to him until now. He pointed out, quite accurately, that my ex was a gold digger. We had a huge fight; I kicked him out of my wedding rehearsal, and in a snit, he flew back to Paris that night, missing my wedding entirely.

Which wounded me more than his eventually correct assumptions that Timothy was wrong for me.

Staring now into the dark, with the sound of the sea crashing to rocks somewhere not very far away, our fight suddenly seemed absurd. He'd tried to contact me several times, but I'd steadfastly avoided him.

Why had I felt so betrayed?

The answer, lurking somewhere in my memories of Arran, suddenly felt too dangerous. The one thing I most certainly did not need was two-bit psychology. I had enough problems.

Beneath me, the engine still rumbled quietly, apparently unhurt. The weather seemed to be easing. I realized I'd been staring out the windshield, waiting for my heart to slow down, and I could actually see out for most of the swipe of the wipers.

Improvement, anyway.

On such a grim night, I wasn't terribly worried about traffic coming up on me one direction or the other, but it was better to get moving anyway. I turned the car around and headed, at a moderate pace, toward the north once again. It wasn't great, but it was a lot better. The car seemed to be all right, despite the bumps and bangs she'd taken the past hour.

I patted the dashboard. "Sorry, baby. You deserved better."

In my coat pocket, my phone suddenly started to ring. I grabbed it and pushed the speaker function. "Make it quick, it's pissing rain and I'm driving."

Paul's voice came through, staticky, but audible. "Sylvie, is Luca with you?"

"What if I said he's right here beside me?"

"Stop playing games. Is he or not?"

I flushed. "Not. Long story."

"He is very dangerous, Sylvie."

"Funny, he says the same thing about you."

"I will admit this was not the most straightforward way of attaining a prize," he said. "But you know I am not a killer."

"Neither is Luca."

"Is that what he told you? Who do you think killed Gunnarsson?"

Damn. I'd bought Luca's story, hadn't I? My head ached with the tangled levels of play at work here. "I don't know."

"Sylvie, I know he is the kind of man who makes young women swoon. But be very wary."

"I am, all right? He's not with me."

"I want to help you, Sylvie. Where can I meet you?"

The car shivered on a rocket of rain. "Hold on," I said, and put my concentration on navigating a steep curve. At least the road was heading away from the very edge of the cliffs. "I'm taking the Katerina to the police."

"Are you? Then why are you driving all over the country tonight?"

"I got distracted," I said, and it was true. It was also very plain that exactly what I needed to do was get the Katerina to the Glasgow police. "I'm going to Glasgow now."

Silence met that statement. "You have her?"

"Yes."

"You know it would mean a great deal to me to

hold her for only a moment. Will you give me that chance, Sylvie? I will not ask you to do anything else. Just let me see her, touch her. One hour."

I made a skeptical noise. "Please. You won't hold her for an hour. You'll take off and I won't do anything because you know—"

"What? I know what, Sylvie? Hmm?"

"Stop it," I said sharply. "Luca underestimated me because he doesn't know me. You know better than that. Don't try the charming routine, all right?"

Surprisingly, he laughed. The sound was wildly distracting, and I had to take a breath to keep my attention on the road. Just ahead was a wide spot for letting faster cars pass and I pulled into it so I could talk without killing myself. "I don't have a lot of time, Paul. There's a good chance I'm being followed, and I need to get to Glasgow before I get killed by thugs."

"What are you talking about? What thugs?"

"I don't know. Three guys followed me—or Luca—to my cousin's holiday caravan. You remember Alan McPheator, don't you?"

"Of course. But who were the men who followed you?"

"I don't know, Paul! They broke in, and I took off." The reality of this whole situation was beginning to annoy me, and now that I was away from the heady presence of Luca's luscious voice and beautiful eyes,

I no longer felt any conflict. For lots of reasons, the least of which was my career reputation, I had to get the Katerina to the inspector in Glasgow. "Look, I'll call you later, all right?"

"Sylvie," he said, and there was command in the word. "Will you let me see it? One hour, I promise you."

"What will that do, Paul? Except frustrate you?"

"You know better. It will please me. I will not ask you to compromise your values. I will not stand in your way if you must take it to the police. It is only that I have gone to a great deal of trouble to find this gem, and I only wish….the intimacy of holding it, seeing it. I know you understand that."

A thousand things were pounding through me—Luca's curls and smell of oranges, my reputation, hanging now by a very slim thread indeed, the lingering low roar of airplane engines that seemed to always take a day or two to go away.

As counterpoint, there was Paul's liquid voice, a narcotic that spun over the bones of my spine, easing the tension at each little bump. I sighed, pressed my head to the steering wheel. "I don't how the thugs found me," I said. "This is also a jewel with a pretty serious curse, you know. Maybe I just want to get rid of it." I laughed without much humor. "You know me and curses."

Again there was a long quiet at the end of the line. This one went so long I said, "Are you there?"

"I am here, *mon petit chou*. I was thinking that it is wonderful to hear your voice again. I have missed you. Terribly."

"I know," I said in sudden honesty. "Me, too."

"Have you forgiven me?"

I thought of our huge scene, in front of the small, quaint church in San Francisco. "Yes. It wasn't you anyway."

He chuckled. "I know."

"Don't get cocky on me, huh?" I looked in the rearview mirror. Still nothing but darkness. "I have to go, Paul."

"Do not go home without seeing me this time, huh? Jewel or no, let me buy you supper one night while you're in Europe? I am staying this week at my cottage on Arran. Come visit me."

"Arran! What are you doing there?"

"I knew you would be in Scotland, Sylvie. Your grandmother told me."

A hard, painful flash of a gorse-covered field on a rocky cliff, myself at seventeen, sent a fist into my chest. "Paul, I don't—"

"You are still angry with me."

"No! I mean, I probably am, but not for the reasons you—"

Lights were coming up behind me, and a sudden tenseness rose in my chest. In a split second, I had to decide: flip the lights off and let the car pass, or take off and try to outrun them on these bad roads if it turned out to be the thugs.

"Sylvie?"

"I think have company," I said, and turned off the lights.

The thugs had been driving a small dark car, which was all I'd known about it. It was hard to tell what this was, coming on the road from the south. Small, nothing fancy about the lights. In the rainy dark, however, I couldn't really tell what it was. Maybe it was a Mini, maybe not. Maybe I hadn't even seen a Mini at the caravan. It was hard to know in the darkness and the rain.

At the last minute, I ducked down to make it appear as if the car was empty. A small dodge, but if it worked, a very easy one. Their car was anonymous. Mine was not.

Holding the phone, I said, "I'm going to take the Katerina to Glasgow," I said. "But I'll meet you on Arran first. Only for an hour, Paul, though, I mean it."

"Thank you," he said quietly. "I'll make your room ready in case you'd like to stay."

"I'm not staying, Paul. I'll just stop in and let you see it."

"All right. When will you be here?"

"In the morning, I suppose. I've *got* to get some sleep."

"Tomorrow will be very good, then."

"Don't hang up for a moment, please," I said, peeking my head up to see if the car was the one I thought. It hadn't slowed, didn't appear to be stopping. Maybe I was getting a break, finally.

And maybe that was because I was finally going to do the right thing by taking the jewel to the Glasgow inspector who'd invited me here.

"I am here," Paul said.

"It's okay. I think I'm safe, finally." I paused. "Thank you."

"My pleasure. Good night, Sylvie," Paul said.

The phrase brought back a thousand memories. I pushed them down into their box. "Goodbye," I said, and hung up.

Then I started the car and headed north once again. There were still monsters about. It would do to be careful.

# Chapter 12

Marbode, Bishop of Rennes (1061–1081), wrote "De gemmarum," on the spiritual and medicinal attributes of gems. In a book lacking in the expected Christian symbolism, Marbode describes diamond: "This stone has aptitude for magical arts, indomitable virtues it provides the bearer, nocturnal spirits and bad dreams it repels, black poisons flee, disputes and screams are changed. Cures insanity, strikes hard against enemies. For these purposes the stone should be set in silver, armored in gold, and fastened to the left arm."

The weather settled a bit into a normal sort of rain. I thought of my father and wondered again where he might be staying. I could use a little advice. Not that he'd ever been particularly wise, you understand, but I could be fairly sure he had no hidden agenda. That was a lot more than could be said of anyone else in this little drama.

I thought of Luca and I wondered if he was still alive.

I thought of the Katerina, tucked into my bra, and all the trouble she'd gotten me into.

I thought of Paul and the summer I was fifteen and about the awful school year in Brazil when I learned to fight.

At the end of that academic year, Paul arrived to whisk me away to his apartment in Paris. I was exhausted and withdrawn, tense as a street cat. Which I suppose, in some ways, I'd become.

Paul was furious with my father for neglecting me so, but in his defense, my father was in terrible condition himself, swirling downward in a spiral of self-destruction. I don't remember if he raced—he must not have, since I was staying with him in Rio. There was a woman at the start, then quite a lot of them, all lush, ethnic beauties who were nothing like my slim, pale Scottish mother.

It's hard to remember, too, how Paul discovered my plight. Perhaps my grandmother was worried about me—she repeatedly asked my father to let me come live with her, go to school in Ayr, have regular meals and a regular life, but he wouldn't hear of it—and sent Paul to investigate the situation. Perhaps he only visited and made sense of it himself. I have no memory of it. The year is a blur of survival challenges.

It would make a good television show—*Reality: Rio Girl Gangs*.

Ha.

Somehow, anyway, Paul discovered the miserable truth of my situation. That we were living in a hovel, and I was virtually on my own in a city of millions, attending a school at which I did not know the language and the girls beat me up on a regular basis, with the meanest of girls right in my own building.

I still want to kill them, those girls, though perhaps I owe them a great debt. They made me tough.

Paul sent me an airline ticket to Paris at the end of the term and I flew in on a Tuesday in May. He picked me up at the gray airport on a soft sunny morning. I had brought little with me—most of it shoved from my drawers into an oversized rucksack—and I was jet-lagged, heart-sore, soul-ragged. I felt like an orphan.

He stood there waiting in the gray, grim, cigarette-stained airport with its Jetson styling, tall and loose-limbed in a pale green cambric shirt that showed off the warmth of his olive-toned skin. His hair was a little long, wavy in the back, the dark, dark ends just touching his collar. To me, he looked like everything good and safe and real in the world.

My defenses dissolved as I moved toward him, and like a very small girl, I flung myself into his arms and wept. He held me. "Oh, my little Sylvie," he murmured, petting my hair, holding me. "I am so sorry, *ma petite puce,* my little flea, so sorry we did not see sooner."

Embarrassed suddenly at this show of emotion, which was very unlike me in those days, I tried to pull away. "I'm all right."

Putting his big, raw-boned hands on my face, Paul said, "You do not have to pretend now, Sylvie," he said. "Not with me." He frowned. *"Oui?"*

I nodded. *"Oui."*

He kissed my brow, took out a white handkerchief and wiped my tears. "Come," he said, "you will eat and sleep and not worry about a thing."

"All right." I kept my head down as he took my bag and we headed out into the brilliance of a French spring. The sunlight felt as delicate as butterfly wings, and there was a scent of grass in the air. I stopped, let the sun touch my face, let the scents of diesel and roses and Paul himself fill me up.

"I love France," I said. "I never want to live anywhere else again."

He touched my arm. "Come. You are worn out." He settled me in his Jaguar, a low black bullet of a car. In every detail, it was built for speed and control, one of the only possible cars for a man who once had raced at extremely high speeds on dangerous courses and nearly killed himself doing it.

By then, I'd learned to love things about cars. This one had a wooden dash. I ran three fingers over the silky smoothness of it. "Sweet."

He gave me a sideways grin. "Indeed…"

By the time I got to Troon, I was cold, wet, grouchy and not in the mood for any bullshit from anyone, an attitude that no doubt cloaked me as I entered the pub. Certainly no one bothered me. It was old and agreeably dim, with a heavy wooden bar and a few businessman-golfer sorts telling tales of their games.

I took a table well away from the bar, and shrugged out of my wet coat. A girl with her hair dyed an unrelenting shade of black came over to take my order. Her skin was the color of a carp.

I ordered tea. "And would you happen to have a pen and a piece of paper I could use?"

Her pencil hovered over a tiny tablet. "Noffin to eat?"

My whole body felt chilled. "Have you got a bowl of soup?"

"We do." Happy to have something to put on her tablet, she laboriously—tongue involved—wrote it down. "Be right back."

Which she was, bearing a welcome steel pot and cup, and a yellow legal pad with two pens. "Will that work?"

"Yes, thank you."

"Are you American?" she said.

It was never a question I quite knew how to answer. "My father is," I said. "And I live there now." Sometimes people are still charmed. "San Francisco."

"Oh, I'd love to go there." It sounded more like *ach, eye'd luve to goooo th'r.* "It looks beautiful."

"It is. You should go someday." I could see she would stand and talk all day, but there was a lot I needed to sort out. "Thanks," I said, and smiled.

She took the hint. "I'll bring your soup out when it's done."

On the paper I drew three columns, one for Paul, one for Luca, one for me. Paul's story was that Luca was a dangerous criminal who would kill for what he wanted. Luca's story was that Paul was a dangerous criminal who would kill to get what he wanted. I didn't think either of them would kill me, and I was fairly certain Paul was not a killer of anyone.

What was bothering me was whether Paul had had anything to do with the first thug in my hotel room. Had he sent someone there to find the diamond, so he could sidestep me in the process?

It illuminated certain questions I'd always avoided asking myself. Paul had always been rich, but I had no idea how he earned that money. It had not been inherited, that much I did know—he'd had a very tough childhood in the industrial city of Lyons. Some of it had likely come from the purses he'd won racing, but it had gone long beyond that now.

So, how did he earn his living? Why had he been mixed up with a notorious drug lord at any point? I wondered if my father would tell me, if he even knew. In another hour or two, I would be able to call him.

One thing that was not in dispute was the fact that Paul had engaged Luca's services to steal the jewel from Gunnarsson. What was less clear was whether Luca had always intended to steal it for himself, or had indeed planned to take it to Paul.

It also seemed plain that Luca had chosen me at some point early in the process, maybe even before he'd stolen the jewel. If he'd known ahead of time that he was going to double-cross Paul, I would be an obvious choice to pull into the situation—not only a jewel expert, but also someone Paul would be reluctant to endanger.

The one element I still didn't understand was the thugs. Who had hired them? The clearly visible answer seemed to be someone connected to Gunnarsson, someone who would know about the jewel.

Or perhaps I didn't want to think about it being Paul.

I poured tea and stirred in milk, rubbing my forehead. What difference did it make in the end? I couldn't trust either one of them, and my obligation lay to the police here in Scotland. They'd hired me to assess the rest of the collection. My integrity was on the line.

The same thing had happened in Egypt last summer. Not the exact scenario, but one where I'd found myself in possession of a great jewel. That one I'd tracked down and managed to return to its rightful place, but I'd encountered some…er…resistance along the way. As with all such jewels, there were those who wanted it for themselves.

I sipped the hot, strong tea. Sylvie Montague, Liberator of Jewels. It had a nice ring to it.

Discreetly, I touched the Katerina below my blouse. Maybe she was simply being liberated here. Maybe the horrific history attached to her needed to somehow be put to rest. On some level, I believed Luca's story about taking the jewel home. It was his very real dread that gave me insight, that and the sense that a jewel thief might feel a lot of respect for a jewel of this much magnificence.

Okay, so: Luca wanted to take Katerina to Romania, where she would end up in a celebrated spot safely behind glass. Luca would be a hero, like his martyred father.

Paul wanted the jewel because he was a collector of beautiful things—paintings, jewels, women. Because he'd heard the story as a boy and yearned to see it, and then his father—not a martyr by any stretch of the imagination, but a petty thief with few graces—had died after taking possession of it.

In a way, I suppose Paul wanted redemption, too. He'd wanted to own the Katerina as long as I could remember. He'd told me stories about it from the time I was small. "Sylvie," he would say, "imagine... a diamond with a ruby inclusion! The ruby is said to be a full carat."

I had a reputation to uphold, but I was also neatly torn. I would not mind helping Luca take the jewel to Romania. I also wanted to deliver it to Paul—to see his face when he held the Katerina. I was not immune to the beauty and lure of the gem.

But if I wished to continue to work in assessment, there was only one right answer. I had to follow the law. I had an obligation to the Scottish police.

Besides, if I morally rearranged facts to suit what I wanted, rather than to do what was right, I'd be just like my father, like Paul and Luca and the rest of the world. Maybe it was just the Catholic in me, but I hated that whole idea of relative morality—it gave people too many excuses to do the wrong thing and call it right.

In this case, it was possible there was a higher moral ground here—that this particular jewel did belong to Romania and should, thus, be delivered there—but that wasn't my decision to make.

From my wallet, I took a card. It was late, but not so late I'd feel bad calling a police inspector's work line. Surely I'd be able to leave a message. On my cell phone I dialed the number.

Voice mail picked up. In a heavy Glasgow accent, a burly male voice said, "You've reached Inspector Barlow. Please leave your message at the beep."

"Hello, Inspector," I said, "this is Sylvie Montague, and I've come into possession of a jewel that is part of the collection you want me to assess. I've had a little trouble tonight, but I'm safe now and should be able to bring it in tomorrow afternoon." I left my cell number and hung up.

The girl was coming to the table with my soup. With a flourish, she put it in front of me, a steaming broth with a hearty scent of beef. Bits of onion floated in it, and she'd brought a good piece of bread and some butter to go with it. "Anythin' else?" she asked.

"No, thanks."

"Ye look so familiar to me," the girl said. "You're not an actress or somethin' are you?"

Ah. "Not exactly," I said with a chuckle. "My father is a Formula One driver. Sometimes, when he's winning, photographers sort of follow me around."

The girl raised her brows. "Well, now, that's something. Do they bother you?"

"Yes. Often." I buttered my bread, picked up my spoon.

The cell phone rang. Thinking it was probably Paul again, I snatched it up. "Excuse me," I said to the waitress. I flipped open the phone. "Hello?"

"Is this Sylvie Montague?" said a male voice with a heavy Scottish accent.

"Speaking."

"This is Inspector Barlow, Glasgow. I just received your message."

"Hello, Inspector. I'm glad you called. I—"

"You're in a bad spot, girl. Is it Katerina's Blood you've got? Half the world is going insane looking for it."

"I'm not surprised. I'll bring it in tomorrow morning."

"You should come tonight."

I shook my head, stirred the soup around. "That's not possible, I'm sorry."

"Where are you, Sylvie? Let me send some protection at least."

Jeez. It seemed like everyone and their brother got weird when it came to this diamond. "No, thank you. I can handle myself, trust me."

"You don't know the kind of people I'm speaking of, young lady."

"I do, sir, and I'll be all right. Thank you for your concern. I'll see you tomorrow, and we can get started." Before he could protest again, I hung up.

Maybe it was just the phone call making me

paranoid, but I suddenly realized that if Luca had managed to get away from the guys back at the caravan, he would be meeting me here. We'd agreed to meet here, but I didn't know if I could deal with him again.

When in doubt, run.

## Chapter 13

The diamond was also used for some time as medical aid. One anecdote, written during the Dark Ages by St. Hildegarde, relates how a diamond held in the hand while making a sign of the cross would heal wounds and cure illnesses. Diamonds were also ingested in the hope of curing sickness. During the early Middle Ages, Pope Clement unsuccessfully used this treatment in a bid to aid his recovery.

—www.costellos.com.au

I jumped up, throwing a five-pound note on the able. "Sorry," I said. "I have to go right now."

Grabbing my things, I headed out into the night. The rain was turned off for the moment, leaving the air damp and freezing, and I shivered as I headed to the car. My hands were burning with cold, and I made a mental note to buy some gloves before getting on the ferry tomorrow.

Rushing for the car, I paid no attention to a small dark, mud-splattered vehicle pulling into the car park until the window was rolled down and Luca was smiling at me. "You're safe!" he said. "Where are you going?"

For a moment, I floundered. "I didn't think you were coming."

"Well, here I am." He nodded. "Climb in," he said, cocking his head toward the passenger seat. "If we drive this, we will be less conspicuous."

I wasn't about to let him get me all tangled in this again. "No, Luca. The Romeo is right over there," I said. "I'll drive."

"Very well. I will park."

As calmly as I was able, I crossed the car park and opened the Romeo's driver-side door. Luca was parking by the lamppost, and I got in the car, started the engine and pretended to be waiting for him.

Just in case, I leaned over and checked the door locks. Good.

Seat belt, good.

Rain, starting to fall again a little——even better.

I backed out of the parking space, and spied Luca crossing the gravel lot with his head down. I put the car into first gear—

And peeled out. In the rearview mirror, I saw Luca run for his own car. *Good luck, buddy,* I thought, and pulled out onto the A-77.

He was behind me in moments. The roads were wet and dark once we pulled out from town a little way. I thought of my father, coaching me on the high mountain roads around San Francisco. My body settled into the seat, my limbs melding into the organic nature of the car around me, not a thing made of metal and glass, bolts and rubber, but an entity of breath and beauty, power and life.

We moved, the pair of us, into the night, like horse and rider dashing over the fields. The car hugged the road, smoothly, climbing and turning, responding without a quiver to my every command. We'd come to know each other, this little car and I, and in spite of my exhaustion, I felt a surge of exhilaration.

Admirably, Luca mostly stayed with me, lagging a little behind, then catching up. He cornered marvelously well, a driver who had some mountain time on him, I'd guess. That was generally how a person came by that clear sense of the center of the road.

Intriguing. I thought of him at the table, reading my palm. Thought of his kiss, so surprising and hot, delicious mouth and skilled, probing tongue. I thought of his hands in my hair, his thumbs on my face. A cradling gesture in which some tenderness lurked.

Minor royalty. What did that mean? I imagined him in a formal blue outfit, with a red sash, his hands in white gloves. And there was me, next to him, a gossamer vision in a ball gown in some giant, gilt-finished room.

The rational part of my brain threw a large stop sign up, and had to chuckle. How ridiculous!

Remember, said that rational side, he's a criminal. A criminal who had set me up and used me and landed me in more hot water than I'd encountered in a long time.

He flashed his lights at me. Once. Twice.

"Forget it, buster."

I sped up. Time to shake him. I stepped on the gas, hard, and headed around the bend. He clung for a little while, then started to slip behind, no match for the Romeo and me.

I had his headlights in view when they sailed crazily to the left, out of control, as I'd been earlier. I swore, and slammed on the brakes, pulling off to one side. Luca's car slammed to a stop against what appeared to be a boulder, hard enough I saw sparks fly out of the body. Maybe, I judged, a broken axle.

Good. I stepped on the gas, headed toward Ardrossan and the ferry in the morning.

But I had not driven even a kilometer before guilt began to eat at me. What if he'd been injured?

*He deserved it*, argued a voice in my head.

Yes, but I'd witnessed the accident, and therefore shared some responsibility.

*Not if he's chasing you with the intent of stealing the jewel again.*

*Sylvie,* said my mother's voice, *you know what you should be doing.*

With a sigh, I turned around. If he bled to death out there, I'd never forgive myself.

The car was exactly where I'd left it, the headlights aimed crazily toward the sea, illuminating the falling rain. With a sense of dread, I suddenly wondered if he'd been killed.

Sliding the Spider into a narrow spot next to the dark blue—Audi? Fiat?—I jumped out of the car. Rain immediately soaked my hair and face and shoulders, and the crash of the sea against some rocks lent a sense of dark drama to the scene. The car engine made no sound, but as I came closer, I could hear it ticking as it cooled. Though the window, I saw Luca's head, still resting against the driver window.

"Luca!" I cried, and yanked open the door. He tumbled out sideways, and his limp body would have fallen into the mud at my feet if I hadn't caught him. I grunted, catching the dead weight of his shoulders on the strength of my thighs.

His face was smeared with blood, but it was unclear whether it was from the earlier wound, which had lost its bandage, or some other injury I couldn't see.

"Luca?" I said more gently. Rain washed the gore away from those lovely cheekbones. His eyelids quivered. I touched his neck, feeling for a pulse, and found it. Not dead, then.

"Luca?" I lightly slapped his face. "Luca, come on, you have to wake up."

He came to with a shuddering, flailing gasp. I caught him before he threw himself by accident over the cliff. "Take it easy!"

He fell on his knees, choked, grasped my wrist. "What happened?"

"You wrecked the car."

Wincing, he looked at the car. Then at the sea. Then me. "You came back."

I nodded, let go of a breath. "Don't ask me why."

"It does not matter," he said. "Thank you."

The car—I could see it was an Audi now—was smoking and obviously not drivable. One of the wheels was cocked at a bad angle.

"What now?" Luca said.

"Let's go. I'll give you a lift to Ardrossan, but then you're on your own."

He nodded, still bent over. "Thank you."

"No argument? Nothing?" I didn't trust him for a second.

He turned away from me, and without drama, vomited. He held up a hand. "I am not feeling well."

I scowled. Didn't vomiting like that mean something? I couldn't remember. "You might have a concussion, but I'll be damned if I know how to check."

"I will be all right," he said, and made his way heavily toward the Spider. "Some day I would like to again have dry clothes."

"Ditto. Let's get out of here."

In the car, I had a moment of foreboding. He put his head back against the seat, and it showed his throat, the elegant cut of his mouth. Even through the damp, I could smell him, a phenomenon so odd I didn't know what to do with it.

He reached out with one hand and captured mine. "Why did you run from me, Sylvie?"

"I don't want to be part of this anymore."

He nodded. One eye slammed closed, as if he had a stabbing pain. "I see."

For a moment, what I wanted to do was smooth a hand over his brow, brush his hair away from his face. My fingers knew how thin the flesh on his cheekbones would feel, how arched and strong the bridge of his nose. There were prickles of dark hair showing across his upper lip, and across his chin, and I imagined what that roughness would feel like across my throat, over the delicate skin of my breasts.

*Get a grip.* He was just another in a long line of men I'd label Big Mistakes. Hadn't I had enough of this sort?

Grimly, I started the car. All I had to do was ignore

the lure of Luca for another hour or two, and then we'd part company for good. No freaking way I was going to head down the road to a fresh broken heart.

And a little voice, the cynical observer, knew none of this was about Luca anyway. It was all about Paul.

It was always about Paul.

Luca fell asleep, and in the darkness, I drove, thinking again of the summer I spent in Paris after my father fell apart.

After picking me up at the airport, Paul took me home to the apartment he kept in the Marais, that section of Paris left untouched by Napoleon's sweeping modernizations. The rooms I knew so well—for we had stayed there often—took up half the fourth floor, and all of the fifth, in an old building, with rooms tucked under the ribs of the old beams. The dormers looked out to a secret courtyard full of roses that were tended by a fierce woman who rarely spoke.

It was a place I had loved from the first moment I'd stepped within, and "my" room, the guest room that opened onto the roofs of Paris, was my favorite of all. When I lay in the bed to read the afternoons away, pigeons cooed along the edges of the roof, and sometimes a giant gray cat wandered in through the windows, sleepy from his hunting. He'd sleep on my knees, purring if I even moved a toe. I never did find out who actually owned him.

For the first few weeks, I withdrew into the deep, soft splendor of my bed, and ate whatever the housekeeper, Brigitte, a thin, sharp older woman, brought to tempt me: little cakes from her oven, cheeses as ripe as noon, eggs shirred and stirred and scrambled and fried, rich cream soups. I would emerge and eat, then dive back into my cocoon again.

My father called, dutifully, every day. He apologized, over and over and over, until I wearied of it and told him to stop or I would not talk to him anymore. I heard Paul reprimand him, as well, a gruff order to pull himself into some reasonable shape.

Finally, when I'd rested a little, Paul pried me out of the room beneath the dormers, and we began a regime that would last the summer. Mornings, rain or shine, we wandered out to a tiny open café no larger than a matchbox. The counter was black with age, the proprietor a ruddy-faced man with a thick mustache. The customers were an assortment of people from the neighborhood, a white-haired old gentleman who looked as frail as spun glass and his tiny, wizened wife; a pair of men who were obviously gay; a pretty career girl with long legs and an impressive bust who brooked no flirtation.

In that little café, we drank café crèmes and ate chocolate croissants carried from the bakery. As I sat at the tiny bar and listened to the flow of French around me, I watched the vendors set up their produce—

plump blueberries and strawberries as big as my hand, piles of spinach leaves and fresh mushrooms. "Why does it all look so much more delicious here?" I asked Paul.

He lifted one elegant shoulder. "It is Paris. Everything is more beautiful here."

"The women are beautiful," I said, "but not as beautiful as in Rio."

When Paul laughed and repeated my English words to the others in French, they laughed with him. I did not look at them, did not care about their opinion. These women were thin and dashing, it was true, but the women in Rio—

"The women in Rio have more passion," I said, in French.

"Ah, no, cherie," said Paul. "There are no more passionate people in the world than the French."

I shrugged. "It does not concern me. Passion is for fools."

Paul looked at me for a long moment. "My poor Sylvie," he said at last, and brushed my cheek with his fingers. "You have been wounded young. As was I."

"You were?"

He inclined his head, straightened. "A story for another day, no? Let's find our pleasure for today."

In the afternoons, we would take in a museum or walk in a park or through some neighborhood or another.

As the weeks ambled by, all in the same easy rhythm, it seemed there was nothing for Paul to do but ferry me to museums, to old houses, to little shops where he bought me baubles and scarves and toys. I had not played tourist in France, and he took delight in showing those sights to me—we went on field trips to Versailles, to Giverny to see Monet's gardens, to Normandy, where soldiers had come ashore, one of them my grandfather, so long ago.

Or so it seemed to me. Paul was amused. "Ancient history, no?"

"It is a long time ago," I said.

He stood on the beach and looked down the long, once-bloodied stretch of it. "When I was a boy, they still spoke of the war all the time. In every village church were the names of the men who had died. In every square was a plaque telling the story of some villager who had been in the Resistance and been killed by firing squad."

"How sad!" I cried.

"If we do not remember what such a war costs," he said, touching my nose, "we are doomed to repeat it, no?"

The only flaw in the ointment that lazy, healing summer was Mariette, Paul's mistress, a woman as sharp-limbed as a grasshopper, with enormous dark eyes and yards of dark hair. She wore scarves artfully, carelessly draped around her neck or shoulders, and smoked cigarettes ceaselessly. Had I been a few years younger, she could have fussed over me, done my nails and hair, bought me training bras. As it was, I was emerging—too quickly—into my womanhood, and my tall leggy body was more from my American father than my French-Scottish mother.

Mariette did not like my living in the apartment. She pouted and protested. She said it was unseemly.

I tried to woo her. It wasn't as if I didn't know how to do it. My father had had, by then, a dozen or so mistresses. It made my life easier if I worked my way into their favor. Sometimes I asked to brush their hair or wished aloud to be as pretty as they were, as well-developed.

Mariette could not be wooed. She was threatened and jealous and made my life miserable in dozens of tiny ways.

When I think of her now, I realize what a small-minded person she was, but then, all I knew was another slam, and she saw to it that I felt betrayed by Paul.

It happened this way. The last week before I was to join my father, who had finally dried out, cleaned up and was living back in San Francisco, Paul made it a point to spend as much of each day with me as he could take from his businesses.

We picked our favorite spots and visited each one—the French crown jewels in the Galerie d'Apollon, and then to a café across the way that had the very best hot chocolate on the planet, served in china cups in a room so bright with gilt and mirrors that one could barely look at it. We ate crepes—mine chocolate, Paul's ham and soft Gruyere—from a stand nearby Ste. Chapelle, a church with splendid stained glass, on a bench on the Ile de Cite, where we watched tourists and housewives march along with their shopping on their arms and the businessmen in good suits annoyed with them both.

The evening before my departure, Paul meant to give me a lovely evening out. I would be sixteen soon, he said, and it was time I had the pleasure of a fine dinner on the town. My birthday was in August; Paul said he and my father would take me to supper as the young lady I was becoming, and then my father and I would return to our base in San Francisco.

I didn't want to go back with my father. For the first time since my mother's death, I had been very happy. I determined there must be some argument I could find to convince everyone that it would be a good idea for me to stay. As the date neared, I thought carefully.

In the meantime, Paul had other activities planned. First, he took me shopping for a dress. Mariette offered to do it, but he refused and I was secretly very pleased.

It was that outing when I began to understand how my feelings had shifted over the summer. We had been shopping. Late summer light turned the bricks of the buildings a rosy golden shade, and there tourists and youths crowding the streets. I carried a tiny handbag made of knotted antique ties.

We paused to join a crowd gathered around a mime performing with two cats. It was astonishing and delightful—the man was clearly fond of his tabbies, and they of him. Who knew cats could be trained? I was amazed by them, and so was Paul, and we were laughing and laughing at them. He put his arm around me, in a friendly way, and gave a little squeeze to my shoulder, pressed a kiss to my temple, as he had a thousand times before.

And—who knows why—it was different. I was suddenly, acutely conscious of his hand on my arm, of his lips against my temple, of a sudden, irrevocable shift of life as I knew it, as if everything on earth had abruptly slid to the left.

I closed my eyes against it, my face flushing. I'd known this feeling. I was nearly sixteen, after all, and had had my fair share of crushes and "boyfriends" here and there. I'd even kissed some of them, and there had been one in Rio, a protector, who had kissed my throat, then my breasts, and I'd enjoyed it very much.

So the sudden flush of awareness toward Paul alarmed and upset me. I tried to block it out. He did not seem to notice anything awry, and there were only a few days left until my departure. I was shocked and ashamed.

And conversely, as hungry to spend time with him as I ever was. I read aloud to him in the evenings as he sorted through paperwork and organized his collections. I ate with him as always, each morning running down the stairs to the bakery for croissants.

I wanted our dinner for my birthday. In my own mind, even if it was wrong, I could have my little fantasy of a handsome prince taking me to the ball.

I'd given up many things in my life.

Not this.

## Chapter 14

The popularity of diamonds surged during the Middle Ages, with the discovery of many large and famous stones in India, such as the Koh-I-Noor and the Blue Hope. Today India maintains the foremost diamond polishing industry in the world.

—www.costellos.com.au

What felt like a dozen years later, my arms and shoulders were burning with exhaustion as I pulled into the grim industrial town of Ardrossan. It was quiet, though not entirely shut down for the night.

Maybe feeling the slowing of the car, Luca sat up, blinking. "Where are we?"

"Androssan," I said. "End of the line for you."

He grunted, pressed fingers to his right eye.

As we passed through the center of town, I spied a filling station that was still, by some miracle, open. "I have to get some petrol. We'll see about hotels there."

He nodded.

I pulled into the station. A man in a plaid jacket was filling the tank of what was obviously a work truck. He looked done in. Tugging the emergency brake, I glanced at Luca, thinking about asking him to fill the tank while I went inside, but one glance was enough. He looked awful, his skin the color of egg whites, his cropped dark hair clumped with dried blood.

Maybe it was dangerous for him to have come anywhere near the Katerina. He wasn't even holding on to it and he was getting pretty battered. "I'll be right back."

I looked the car over, wincing at the long scratches on the right, the dent on the left fender where I'd smashed the side of the hill when I spun out. Mud splatters marred the red paint, and the driver's side window was smashed from Frankenstein's fist.

Vaguely, I thought again, where were these guys coming from? Who sent the thugs?

But I couldn't really hold the thought. I was too

tired. Taking the nozzle out to fill the tank, my arms felt like they weighed 10,000 pounds each.

Or maybe that would be 10,000 tons.

The liters clicked away, adding up obscenely, and I resolved, as I always did, to never complain again about the price of gasoline in America. The overhead fluorescents beat down on the scene with their usual depressing cast, and I huddled into my damp coat, putting my back to the icy wind. I glanced at Luca through the windshield, and he had his eyes closed.

Could it only have been six hours since we'd met?

Inside, the clerk was obviously performing the last tasks of the day, wiping down the counters, straightening the stock.

"Hi," I said, stomping off the chill.

She nodded and went back to her tasks. From the counter, I picked up a couple of bottles of water and a packet of chocolate biscuits and handed them over. I pulled out a credit card to pay, and realized with a cold shiver that it would be a way to track me if someone was inclined. "Wait," I said. "I'll pay cash."

"Thank you," she said, taking the notes.

"Is there a hotel close by?"

She had hair as shiny red as a setter, which she flipped away from her thin face. "Ye can try the Carrick B&B." She gave me directions.

"Thanks," I said, depositing my change.

Back in the car, Luca stirred when I opened the

door, rousing himself. I gave him a bottle of water, feeling a wreck with my wet hair and wet feet and makeupless face. "I hate not having my things," I said, looking into the rearview mirror and poking at my hopeless hair. My lips were as pale as chalk. "Ugh."

His smile was half-hearted as he unscrewed the lid of the water. "You're lovely even when you look like a drowned cat."

"At least I don't look dead, like some people in this car."

"*Un*dead, remember. I am from the land of Count Dracula."

"Ah, I knew I should have recognized that accent."

We drank water silently for a minute. "Do you want me to get out now?" Luca asked.

"It would be best," I said, "but I don't seem to have the heart to make you do it."

He looked at me. "No?"

"Don't get any ideas." I put the water bottle down and fit the key into the ignition. "I can't turn you out on the streets when you're bleeding and exhausted, but it's not because I'm entertaining thoughts of bliss in your arms."

"You have a sharp tongue!"

"Aye," I said wryly in Scottish. "Just so ye understand I ken yer motives."

"Do you?" he asked quietly. "I wonder if you do."

"You can't bear to touch this jewel. You want me

along to be your courier." I frowned. "Not that it seems a particularly good idea for you to be this close to it. Have you noticed?"

That startled him. "I had not thought of that."

"Yeah, well, maybe it's the curse after all."

"I don't believe in the curse," he said.

"Oh, *really?*" I rolled my eyes.

He blinked lazily. "Do not be arrogant, Sylvie."

"I wasn't. I mean, I just thought…it's your Achellies' heel."

He sipped his water, then nodded. "Perhaps the Katerina is the weakness in my family."

"So why risk it, Luca?" I asked.

He shrugged. "It is, as you say, a long story."

"Okay." I pulled out. "The girl said there's a hotel on the High Street. We should be able to get a room there."

I had to get the proprietor out of bed, and I wisely used my Scottish accent because she was grumpy and xenophobic when she looked out the window and saw the swarthy—and grimy-looking—Luca sitting in the car. "My husband," I said with a wicked lift of my eyebrow. "Handsome, isn't he?"

Her watery blue eyes said she was too polite to disagree to my face. I paid her in cash, and she gave me a key. "Ye don't mind seeing yerself upstairs, d'ye?"

"Not at all."

The room was small, she said, with only one bed— and I couldn't very well complain after saying he was my husband, could I?—but it had an en suite bathroom, and that was a major plus. I thanked her profusely.

Luca barely could walk up the stairs. He had to lean on the railing unsteadily and haul himself up a stair at a time. He must have taken quite a battering in the car accident.

Or, I remembered, at the hands of the thugs. I'd have to remember to ask him what had happened there.

We let ourselves into the room, plain and square and old, smelling of damp plaster and mildew. It was cold. A sagging double bed covered in a white chenille spread from the old days of chenille occupied the place of honor.

But it was very clean. Every surface was dusted and polished, and the curtains were crisply pressed. On the dresser was an electric kettle and a basket of tea bags, individual tubes of sugar and packets of dried cream. Very civilized.

Luca limped into the room and settled with a groan on the chair. I squatted to turn on the fire. "How did you get away from those guys?"

"You took care of one very well, and I got away from the one outside and stole the car."

"So they're still back there, somewhere?"

He lifted his shoulders, let them drop. "What will they drive, hmm?"

In the light, he looked very grim indeed. "Why

don't you go shower?" I said. "It will be warmer when you come out."

"Thank you." He peeled off his coat and spread it over the chair. "For everything, Sylvie. I did not earn it."

"I know."

He disappeared into the bathroom, and I stripped off my own coat and the sweater below it so I could warm up. I shivered there next to the gas flames for a few minutes, but the room did take to warming very quickly. I moved to the mirror.

I looked worse than I expected. So bad, really, that it surprised me that no one had commented. My right eye was a little battered, though not so much as my chin, which had taken the brunt of my fall at the caravan. It was quite purple.

Not to mention, every scrap of makeup I'd put on had been washed away, and I looked about sixteen.

In the bathroom, I heard the water go on, and took the chance to strip off my T-shirt, too, and examine my wounded breast. The Katerina made a nice lump in the silhouette of the bra, and I slipped it out, wincing. It hurt to take it out, and I was afraid to look at the tender flesh. Visible above the fabric of the bra was a finger of red.

It didn't matter—once the jewel was in my hand, I forgot all but the Katerina, all 80 magnificent, humming karats. She captured me, again. The play of light which makes diamonds so appealing was multiplied a hundredfold. Even the most desultory diamond clasps the light, returns it back to you.

And this one—I loved the simple table cut that allowed the rainbows of light to enter and exit with such elegant directness, the quality of sparkle, glints of rainbows. There in the middle, the dark red ruby, suspended like blood, a heart. A tear.

"Where do you want to be, my beauty?" I asked her.

Every jewel, left loose or made into a ring or a brooch or a necklace designed to hang between the breasts of a woman, has a story. The geological story to begin, of course, all those forces coming to bear, transforming elements into something rare and fine.

Then the discovery, the raw ore yielding something huge and impressive to be shaped and sawed and illuminated.

"She has seduced you, hasn't she?" Luca said from behind me.

I jumped—I hadn't even heard the shower turn off!—and covered my chest with my shirt hastily. I needed to put it on, but the idea of trying to straighten the wet fabric was too much to contemplate. Mostly covered, I turned. "Perhaps."

He was shirtless, too, and damp from the shower. His hair, towel-dried into ringlets, made me think of a Renaissance painting. He'd slipped back into his jeans, but the shirt was flung over one shoulder. His chest was beautiful. Supple skin covered toned pecs, and there was exactly the right amount of dark hair scattered in an artful triangle between his nipples.

He came closer and looked at the diamond, careful not to touch it. "I have never seen anything so beautiful," he said.

"I know, I am, aren't I?"

He bent and kissed my shoulder. "You are attracted to me, I think."

"Yes," I said, and moved away from his reach. "But it doesn't matter. You're a criminal and you used me."

His lips quirked in appreciation, and he hesitated, then cocked his head. "Will you mind if I kiss you just once as a real thing, just to see what might have been?"

"I do mind," I said, and picked up the jewel to tuck back into my bra. For a moment, I'd forgotten the injury, and sucked in my breath at the pressure. "Ohh, other side, I think."

"What happened?"

"Nothing much. An encounter with the floor." I vaguely indicated my chin. "No big deal."

"Shall I look at it for you, hmm?"

"Very funny. How's your head?"

"I'm fine." He tossed his shirt on the bed. "I assume we will share the bed?"

"Not much choice, is there?"

He shook his head.

"I'm going to shower," I said.

I felt superstitious about the jewel, and took it into the shower with me. The water was good and hot, and I felt tension and cold and long hours of driving and travel pour down my arms, my legs, and go down the drain. I dried off, then wiped clean a spot on the mirror so I could look at my poor bruised breast.

Not pretty—but it was remarkable. The jewel had left an exact imprint on the white flesh of my breast, a purply-green rectangle. With a star of broken blood vessels in the middle, bright pink.

Eerie. For a long moment, I stared at it, wondering if there was any truth to that curse. Would I, too, meet a gruesome, violent death?

I thought of the thugs again. How had they tracked me to the hotel? To the caravan, which was out in the middle of nowhere? And what—

Stop. I had to get some sleep before anything else happened. Wearily, I pulled on enough clothing to be decent—bra and underwear, basically, and even those were damp, but I'd at least have semi-dry clothes tomorrow morning if I left them all spread out in the room. Tucking the Katerina back into my bra, I carried my T-shirt into the other room and spread it over the night stand, close by the fire.

"Are you warm enough?" I asked Luca, who had climbed into bed and was watching television, one arm propped behind his head. There was something so intimate about the casually exposed hair beneath his arm. I had to look away, an odd heat in my cheeks.

"Finally, yes," he said. "The blankets are warm, too. Come." He clicked off the television with the remote control, and pulled back the covers for me.

I hesitated. What did he have in mind?

## Chapter 15

Scintillation: refers to the flashing and twinkling sparkle of a diamond when moved under
light. A diamond is always more beautiful in
motion because its scintillation depends upon
the number of facets visible to the eye when the
diamond moves.

—www.costellos.com.au

I crawled in gratefully. For the second time tonight, we
curled together. Every cell in my body damned near
wept at the pleasure of lying prone, in a soft place, with
warmth around me. Luca spooned close, his body warm
and solid. "It means nothing," he said, "only comfort."

"All right." I put my arm over his, let my head sink into the pillows. "You are warm. I've been frozen for hours."

"Where is that accent from, Sylvie?"

"I'm American."

"No. There is more." He murmured the words close to my neck, like a long-term lover. "Cannot place it, exactly."

"My mother was Scottish. And the first ten years of my life, we lived between Nice and Ayr, so I picked up parts of both of those accents." I smiled to myself and said, in my best Scottish, "I can speak Scottish when I've a mind to."

He chuckled.

"And," I said with the musical lilt of that language, "I have perfected a French accent for travel in Europe this days, which is better than being American, no?"

"Yes," he said with another small laugh.

"I can even," I said in a posh London accent, "be quite British when the situation requires it."

He went quite still behind me. "Are you Interpol?"

I laughed. "No."

"You should be."

"Too dangerous."

"You've had danger here tonight, no? And weren't you nearly killed in Egypt last summer? It was in the news—The Blue Nile."

"Well, my mother used to say I had a talent for trouble. Last summer, a sheik wanted the Blue Nile as badly as the Egyptian government."

"As now." His hand moved on my tummy, slightly, and his breath touched my ear.

"Yes," I said, and squeezed his wrist to halt his imaginings. "Go to sleep Luca."

"Mmm."

Outside, the rain splayed against the window again. The faint hiss of gas feeding the fire was a comforting sound. Luca spooned around me.

I felt him fall asleep. Heavily, deeply. A moment later, he began to snore very quietly. It made me think of a kitten.

Only then did I allow myself the luxury of letting go. I tumbled hard into the most narcotic of submarine sleeps, so far and deep and away it was like going to another planet.

Awakening slowly, I felt Luca's weight before I fully surfaced, and for long moments, I felt confused and disoriented. Where was I? With whom?

*Paul.*

I'd been dreaming about him, in some wicked way, which was what always seemed to happen if I let down my guard. Next to me, Luca shifted and I surfaced more completely. His hand moved on my arm.

"Are you awake?"

"Sort of," I said, and cleared my throat. "How did you get away from the thugs yesterday, anyway?"

"Same way you did—I just kept fighting."

"I don't understand how they found me."

"I don't know that answer, Sylvie," he said. His hand moved on my hip, which was nearly bare. It felt luxurious, especially when he nestled closer, pressed his lips to the back of my neck. "You feel nice," he said.

"No funny stuff," I said, shifting away. "You've gotta go."

"I could love you," he said.

"Don't be ridiculous."

"I am quite serious. You are beautiful, smart, balanced." He pushed against me. "Will you come to Romania with me, Sylvie? Please?"

A sudden warning told me this was not a game, that I could be in trouble if I didn't play along. For a long moment, I was still, then I turned and put my hand on his lovely face. "Are you really so afraid of the curse?"

"No," he said, "I just want you." He slid his hand upward, and covered my breast, and the jewel. With hooded eyes, he looked at my face. "You want me, too," he said. "I can feel it." He stroked my nipple to arousal, a purely sensory response, and then bent over my mouth. "Don't you?"

I wondered, suddenly, what his game was. I let him kiss me, pretended to be swept away. "I am attracted to you," I said, "but that's not really enough. What's in it for me if I carry the jewel into Romania for you?"

"We can work something out," he said, and drew his hand down my body. Against my thigh, I felt his urgent arousal, and I caught his hand before he went exploring too much.

"Not now," I said. "Let's eat."

I did not have to catch the ferry to Arran until mid-morning, which gave me time to think of what to do to handle Luca. We followed the scent of good Ayrshire bacon down the stairs to the dining room, which was made cheery by green and white chintz and sparkling clean windows. The weather beyond was grim, of course, but it was spring in Scotland. Some daffodils struggled to keep their heads up in a windowbox.

The breakfast was hefty—eggs and bacon, tomatoes and mushrooms, the good fluffy white bread that's practically a lost art in America now, and black pudding. "Want my pudding?" I asked Luca.

He nodded happily. "You do not like it?"

"No, thank you." My head felt much clearer this morning. "So what will you offer me?"

"I'm not doing this for money," he said.

"That's a lie, Luca. It's just that you think you can get something else out of it, too."

"Perhaps." He spread jam on his toast. "What do you want?"

"Half of whatever you get."

He rolled his eyes. "Please."

"Thirty percent, then."

"Twenty."

I pursed my lips. "Twenty-five."

He considered for a long moment. "All right. Twenty-five it is."

My plan was to abandon him at the very next opportunity—he'd have to wash his hands or use the toilet, and that would be that.

Sayonara, Luca.

Unfortunately, we headed back to the room without a chance for me to ditch him.

And more fool I.

I bent down to pick up my bag and felt a blow come down on top of my head. I tumbled forward, stunned, and tried to catch myself before I hit my face again. Too late, my hand slammed into the corner, at least protecting my mouth from that viciousness, and my eyebrow alone caught the door handle to the bathroom.

"I am sorry, Sylvie," Luca said, grabbing me from behind, capturing my wrists in a fierce grip.

"Bastard!" I cried, and slammed my foot backward, trying to catch his instep, but he danced away. He had my wrists stacked one on top of the other, and was now wrapping something around them. I struggled, trying to get away.

"Do not make me hurt you," he said, and with a tensile strength that belied his size, he picked me up, pressed me against the wall, his body against mine. "I do not want to hurt you," he said, and touched my hair. I yanked away, feeling something drip in my eye.

"Damn you."

"No doubt," he said ironically. He put his attention on my ankles, wrapping them tightly together with what I saw now was duct tape. I roared my frustration, and tried to pull my wrists apart.

"Luca, don't do this, please. You said yourself that you'll die if you handle this jewel."

"I went to great trouble to avoid it, but now there is no choice." With a last, satisfied snap, he tore the end of the tape holding my ankles, and stood up. "You wanted payment, and I am not returning it for payment. I am returning it for the honor of my family."

"What does a thief care about honor?"

He turned me around to face him, not ungently. "If there was a monarchy in my country, I would be fifth in line for the throne. But my father disgraced our family through his exploits with the Communists, and I was a hostile youth, you understand?"

I looked at him.

"If I return this jewel, they will make a place for me again. I am tired of wandering."

"So let me help you!"

He shook his head, and with one gentle hand, brushed my hair from my face. "It seems you have charmed me, little Sylvie. I do not wish you to be hurt."

"So you're going to tie me up and leave me here?"

"I wish to make you comfortable," he said.

"Oh, I am so comfortable," I said furiously, my arms trapped behind me, duct-taped firmly together.

"Forgive me, Sylvie," he said, "but I must have the jewel."

He unbuttoned my sweater, then started on my blouse without looking at me. I could see it was not easy for him. His long, graceful fingers fumbled twice, and as my flesh became exposed, I admit, I too, was somewhat rattled by the whole thing. When he spread open my blouse to expose my chest, bra and belly, my breath caught. He noticed. His gaze lingered on my breasts, his fingers brushing lightly against my belly.

Despite the situation—or perhaps because of it— I found myself responding. He still smelled of oranges, and my body still thought him beautiful, and the brush of his hands over my belly as he pushed my blouse out of the way made my nipples leap to attention, the eager little sluts.

Luca noticed. "I wish," he said with regret, "that I had been able to give your beautiful breasts the attention I think they would like from me."

"It's cold in here," I said.

"Ah." He raised his eyes and smiled at me, those teeth flashing white against his beautiful mouth. "Is that what it is?"

"Yes."

"You have no reaction to me at all?"

"No."

"So," he said, moving closer, "if I touch you, all it does is revolt you? If I do this—" he traced a light circle on my belly "—it does nothing for you?"

"Nope."

"What if I bend my head, and take that bold soldier into my mouth? Hmm?"

His hands slid downward, and teased the tops of my breasts. I finally found my voice.

"Get away from me, Luca. You're a liar, a thief, a petty criminal. You're gonna get yourself killed. What would I want with a man like you?"

His laughter surprised me, a low, rich sound, so knowing. "This is what you want, Sylvie," he said, and kissed me.

It was no light, teasing thing. It was an aggressive demand, his mouth and tongue utterly claiming my mouth. I resisted him at first, keeping my mouth closed and tight, but his lips were lush and coaxing, the movements of his body suggestive, softly easing into me, against me, his shirt brushing my bare belly. When he touched my hair, took my face into his hands, I felt a swift tug through my being, and without consciously choosing it, I somehow opened to his kiss. He made a sound, a low groan, and his tongue swirled in, and coaxed mine into a slow, sensual dance.

I could do nothing, hands and feet bound. Instead of protesting, I found myself opening to him.

He groaned and pulled away. "You move me, Sylvie Montague."

I said nothing. He raised his head, looked me in the eye. "I must do this now," he said, and took one small step back so he could lift his hands to my breast, and using one hand, gingerly pulled back the fabric of the bra, reached inside, and withdrew the jewel. When he had it in his hand, he trailed one finger down the slope of my uninjured breast, and bent down to kiss the same spot.

He tucked the jewel into his pocket, then took a moment to button my blouse again, and then put a piece of tape over my mouth and laid me on the bed. "So long, Sylvie."

I glared at him.

He reached into my purse, found my keys and was gone.

# Chapter 16

One of the great jewel heists of the twentieth century occurred during the weekend of February 15-16, 2003, when thieves cleaned out more than two-thirds of the 160 safe-deposit boxes in the highest security centers of an Antwerp Diamond Center. Most of the city's dealers were attending the Diamond Games tennis tournaments, so the robbery was not discovered until the day after the games. The numbers were so high that even weeks later, police had not fully counted the losses. None of the missing diamonds have ever been recovered.

*—Jewel Heists*

I did not lie there long. It was a bed and breakfast, after all, a small establishment. I could have waited for the maid or cleaner to come around, but that would cost precious time—time Luca was rushing away with the Katerina, on his way to Romania.

No doubt driving my car, the bastard.

Wriggling my way to the end of the bed, I lifted my legs and started slamming my heels down against the floor. Over and over—bam, bam, bam. It wasn't long before someone was at the door, keys in the lock. The proprietor came in.

"Oh, God!" she cried when she saw me lying there, trussed with gray duct tape. She rushed over, keys rattling, and bent over, her hands waving. I made a noise, frustrated, and turned to show her my taped wrists.

"Oh, dear!" She reached for the tape on my mouth, and I shook my head violently, pointing with my head to my wrists.

In my purse, my cell phone started ringing. Good grief! What was it about that stupid thing going off at all the worst times?

"D'ye want me to get that?" the woman asked.

"Mmmmm!" I cried behind the tape, knocking my head toward my hands.

She must have misunderstood it as a nod, because she rushed over and picked up the phone, flipping it open and breathlessly saying, "Hallo! Hallo! She's busy just this minute." She listened and said, "Just a minute." To me she said, "He says his name is Paul."

Only I could get rescued by The Three Stooges' little sister. I stopped making any noise, not moving at all, and she got it.

"Sorry, dear," she said, "I don't know what I'm thinking."

At last she reached behind me and pulled the tape off my wrists, then handed me the phone. I yanked the tape off my lips, feeling skin ripping off with it, and barked into the phone, "Hello?"

"Where are you, Sylvie?"

"In a bed and breakfast in Ardrossan. I've had a little delay." Nearby, the proprietor folded and unfolded her hands. I lifted a finger to her, the phone to my ear as I bent to untape my ankles. "Why? I said I'd be there and I will."

"Have you seen the news today?"

"Not yet."

"Two men were found dead at a caravan near Dunure. The police think it was related to the murder of Gunnarsson."

A chill passed over me. "Dead?"

"Where is he, Sylvie? You are in grave danger."

"No, I'm not, actually. I'll be on the next ferry. We'll talk then."

I hung up.

"You need the police?" the woman asked, a

worried frown between her brows, those narrow hands working around in circles.

"No, thank you," I said, shaking off the tape and dropping it in the trash. "This is personal. I'll handle it myself."

"If ye're sure, then?"

"Very," I said, tasting blood. Grabbing my coat and purse from the chair, I said, "Sorry for the trouble," and stalked out.


The ferry dock was close enough I could walk to it, and it was good for my mood to get some exercise. It was crisp and cold outside, threatening rain, but after spending the day wet yesterday, I felt downright toasty warm. Amazing what dry clothes will do for a person's comfort.

The exercise was also good for my mood. Back in San Francisco, I worked out three or four times a week, usually running on the beach or, if it was rainy, on treadmills at the gym. After two days of sitting in planes and cars, my legs and arms were grateful for the movement. I crossed my arms over my chest and strode through the narrow lanes, making my way toward the dock.

Fuming.

I couldn't believe I'd been so stupid. I should have left Luca on the side of the road, in the steaming wreck of car he'd stolen from the thugs he'd killed.

Except….there was something odd about that.

How could Luca have single-handedly killed them? Two guys, not to mention one had been Frankenstein's size. I'd left one in the caravan, injured, but not dead—at least I didn't think so.

Something about it just didn't feel right.

I bought my ticket and sat on a bench outside, watching seagulls circle overhead. One lit on a post nearby and preened as if waiting for his picture to be taken, his white feathers a lovely contrast against the dark purple-gray sky and the rounds of the island in the distance.

Arran. A place of memory and promise, disappointment and embarrassment, magic and mystery.

Quite a lot of people were gathering, and I felt crowded by the numbers. I stood up and walked toward an open spot nearby the ropes, and shook my head.

Why was I bothering to go to Paul when the jewel was stolen? I'd be better off to just follow Luca on my own, try to track him down myself. It was my problem—I'd lost the jewel, and it was my responsibility to get it back. I was no longer a girl, seeking rescue from a champion.

But Paul had money and muscle. He'd do it faster than I could, and I'd have the satisfaction of seeing Luca's face when Paul showed up.

Waves lapped against the shore, and the only sounds about were the birds and the water, and far away, the sound of the whistle. A lonely sound. A lonely place.

There was a hollowness in my chest now, and I stood up, trying to fight it off. Too many memories were warring for precedence, and I refused to let any of my humiliations come up at all.

A girl with a long scarf walked by. The fringes hung down her back, orange and pink, which made me think of the dress I'd worn on my sixteenth birthday.

Paul and I had gone shopping for it in Paris. After the first blaze of awareness of my changing feelings for my guardian, I protected my secret carefully. It was painful and sweet. It kept me awake nights, and lent my days an effervescence I'd never known.

I also knew it was ridiculous, that he was so much older than I, and so much more polished and knowledgeable in every way that I could never hope to capture his attention.

But it was also nothing like my seven-year-old self saying I was going to marry him someday, much to the indulgent amusement of the adults in my world.

It is also true that I was not an ordinary, sheltered sixteen-year-old girl. I'd lived all over the world, and had learned to function in almost any setting. I spoke three languages, had lived on four continents, and could order wine for one or a hundred.

The day we went shopping for my birthday dress, I relished the experience of being alone with him, modeling dresses for his pleasure. We finally settled on a floaty chiffon dress with spaghetti straps that fluttered over my body like a breeze. The pink and orange colors set off my dark blond hair and showed off my tan shoulders. In a pair of high-heeled shoes, I felt like a Parisian.

Afterward, we stopped for a lemonade at a café on the Rue de Sévigné, and as I watched the people parade by in their summer suits and dresses, I found the courage to say, "Paul? May I talk to you about something important?"

He reached for my hand. "Of course. Anything."

I took a breath. "Did you just—um—" I cleared my throat, started again. "Am I a both—" I halted again.

His fingers moved on my hand, his gray green eyes showed concern. "What is it, Sylvie? Is everything all right?"

"I—oh, I just don't know how to say it, so—" I sat up straight and looked him in the eye. "I don't want to go with my father. I want to stay here in Paris and live with you and go to school."

Something bright, then dark, passed over his eyes, too fast for me to read. "You like it here?"

"Yes!" I said fervently. "I think I am happier in Paris than anywhere. Brigitte takes good care of me, and you teach me things all the time, and I think....I don't...." I thought of my life in Rio and had to fight very hard to keep tears out of my eyes and voice. I scowled, hard. Swallowed. "I just want to be here."

He moved his thumb over my thumbnail. "I have always been honest with you, *ma poulette*. I do not know that staying here would be best for you."

"Why?"

With that peculiarly European click of his tongue, he looked toward the shops. "You should go to America, learn that part of yourself."

Stung, I lowered my eyes. Tried to withdraw my hand, but he caught my fingers, smiling at me. "So much pride, my Sylvie. I would be happy to have you stay. You bring laughter and pleasure into my house, but I am not always here—"

"Brigitte is here when you are gone, and at least I know…at least…"

"There is someone at home?"

"Yes."

"Your father has been in a place to dry out this summer, Sylvie. It means the world to him that he should have you back again."

This shamed me. I took a breath. "I know."

He squeezed my fingers gently. "I am delighted that you have found so much to love in Paris, Sylvie. It suits you, this city."

"Does it?"

"Oh, yes." He smiled and straightened, letting

my hand go. "You are welcome to return as often as you like."

I tried not to show my disappointment, but it stung like physical pain, and to my horror, tears welled up in my eyes. Blinking brightly, I tried to nod, then stood abruptly. "I'll be right back."

"Sylvie—"

Blindly, I rushed for the toilet, and once there, let the tears fall as they would, rushing from my eyes in a river that shocked me. I loved Paris, and living in the Marais, and the apartment with its quirky bedroom, and having Brigitte fuss over me was like having a mother around.

But I would not pine for those things, not like I'd pine for the company of my guardian. When I looked back in my life, it seemed those times I was happiest were when he was part of our lives. This summer had only reinforced that tenfold, a hundredfold. I didn't want to live anywhere that I'd face long stretches of not seeing him.

I ran cold water and splashed my face with it gently, then squared my shoulders and met my eyes in the mirror. Crying would not get me what I wanted.

What would?

I didn't know. But I would give it some thought.

As I boarded the ferry, I pushed the memory of that Paris summer away, and snapped my cell phone open.

It was finally a decent time to try to reach my father in Malaysia.

His cell phone rang on the other end. Once, twice, three times. With much disappointment, I thought I wasn't going to get through. I was about to hang up with he answered, "Hey, baby girl! Where are you?"

"Hi, Dad. I'm on a ferry going to Arran. Did you have a practice race today?"

"Not bad. Not great. I finished third, but it's early days yet. What are you doing in Arran?"

"I'm going to see Paul."

"Is that so." It wasn't a question. "Hmph. Thought you didn't talk to him anymore."

"Well, maybe I got over it."

"About time."

I felt stung over that, and had to take a minute to figure out why. "I'm calling to ask you about him, actually."

"Yeah? Like what?"

The questions seemed idiotic now that I was about to phrase them. *Do you think he could be a killer? Do you think he's a high-level crook who had a drug lord murdered?* "Oh, I don't know. Never mind."

"Something bothering you, kiddo?"

"Well, I've sort of gotten mixed up with this big mess of a jewel heist. Paul is mixed up in it, but I'm not sure how."

"Mixed up how, babe? Are you in trouble?"

The last thing I wanted was for him to worry before a race. "No! Not at all. I've called the police and will talk to them this afternoon."

"Good. I heard they called you to Glasgow. I'm really proud of you."

"Thanks."

"How long will you be in Europe? Can we get together? I'm headed to France after this, maybe Paris for a day or two when you're finished?"

"I'd like that. I've got a job lined up outside Lyon in a couple of weeks—it's meant to be a spectacular set of jewels, the mistress of some sixteenth century prince."

My father chuckled, the sound robust and rich, the laughter of a younger man. Racing, he always said, keeps him young. "I'll skip Lyon, but let's plan on Paris, huh?"

"All right."

"And about Paul, kiddo? I'd trust him with my life. More, I'd trust him with yours and I have."

"Thanks, Dad."

"Will you see the race tomorrow?"

"Wouldn't miss it for the world. You know I'm always watching you, Dad."

"I'm always racing for you."

I smiled. "Thanks. Talk to you soon."

## Chapter 17

Not only was it believed that diamonds could bring luck and success, but also that they could counter the effects of astrological events. These myths laid the groundwork for monarchs to begin wearing diamonds as symbols of power. King Louis IX of France (1214-1270) valued diamonds so highly that he established a law reserving diamonds for the king alone.

—www.diamondgeezer.com

I found a cup of tea and took it to the deck to watch the sea, thinking of my father. He wanted to be reliable. He wanted to take care of me.

He just didn't really know how, and that had caused all sorts of chaos in my life. Even the simplest of things—showing up, or rather *not* showing up, for my sixteenth birthday dinner, had held consequences for me, more than him.

Everyone else had made an effort to help me celebrate this birthday—my grandmother had sent gifts early, and they'd been sitting on the table in the foyer for a week; Paul had gone to great lengths to plan an evening that would be glamorous and enjoyable. Brigitte had baked my special favorites, and washed and combed my hair for me. We giggled all day, nibbling sweets, drinking café, trying on jewelry and hairstyles. My father was due at three, and we were all going to go for a leisurely ride on the Seine in a small yacht Paul had borrowed from someone.

My father called at 2:00, just as Brigitte was brushing my hair out into long waves. "Happy birthday, baby!" he cried into the phone.

"Thanks, Dad! Where are you calling from?"

"Well, that's the thing, sweetheart. I'm stuck in the States, still. Can't get there today after all."

"What?" Swords of disappointment sliced through me. Not again.

"Honey, I just couldn't get there. I'm so very sorry."

"I don't understand. Why did you wait so long to call? You had to have known a lot sooner than this."

"I've been trying all day. There was a problem with the first flight—"

"Right," I said, cutting him off. "Whatever. It's always something, isn't it?"

"Honey, I know you're mad at me, but don't be. I'll be there tomorrow or the next day and I'll bring you home to San Francisco. You'll like it. I've got a great apartment in a great old house, and your bedroom will be in the attic, with all these windows that look out toward the bay. You'll love it, I just know it."

"I'm sure I will, Dad," I said, heavily.

We talked for a few more minutes, but I was feeling the first truth of reality regarding my father: I could never expect him to be anything except unreliable. You couldn't get mad at a giraffe for being a giraffe—you had to just accept them as they were.

And I *was* allowed to try to protect myself, make a better life. Somehow, I had to find a way to stay in Paris. Maybe my grandmother could be my ally—as a Frenchwoman, she loved the place herself, and she'd seen how unreliable my father was the past few years. I would give it some thought.

In the meantime, I would enjoy this evening.

Often, I wonder how things would have been different if Mariette had not decided to see us off. I flew down those stairs in my new pumps that made me feel so grown up, and saw Paul through the slats in the stairs, blinking in surprise, then happiness as

I flew across the room in my beautiful dress that he'd chosen.

"You are lovely," he said.

I laughed happily. "Thank you!"

He handed me a small box. "Here is your gift from your old guardian, huh? Open it."

It was a jewel, of course. But not just any jewel—it was a replica of a necklace that had once belonged to the wife of an Indian Raj, made with a deep red pigeon's blood ruby, set delicately on either side with soft pink topazes. "Oh!" I cried, and my hand flew to my mouth. "It's the Princess's necklace!"

He smiled. "A replication, of course, but I was pleased at how beautifully they did it."

"It's beautiful, Paul!" I held it out to him. "Will you put it on for me?"

"It would be my pleasure," he said.

I turned and lifted my hair. Paul came close behind me and I took three seconds to close my eyes and imagine he was my lover, that those strong hands now brushing my bare shoulders would settle on my skin, open-palmed, and he'd kiss my neck.

Of course all he did was fasten the necklace and spin me around so that he could admire it. "Beautiful," he pronounced.

From behind us came the droll approval of Mariette. "My, my," she said dryly, "don't you look grown up tonight!" She looked closely at the neck-lace. "Oh, lovely, lovely."

"Thank you."

"I only came by to bring you some chocolates and say hello to your father—is he here yet?"

"No. He was delayed," Paul said, putting his hand on my elbow. "We shall be late, Mariette. You'll forgive us if we move along."

"Oh, I'm so sorry."

I lifted a shoulder. Not even Mariette could ruin this evening for me. "It's all right."

"Paul, you can't mean to be taking this girl out alone, just the two of you?"

"Not only do I intend to, we are leaving now." He put his hand at the small of my back, and I felt a swelling sense of power as I met Mariette's eyes.

She saw it, too. "Of course. You have planned it for a month, and it is impossible to let it be ruined by her father's bad manners."

"More than that," he said, smiling down at me. "It is her sixteenth birthday. Surely you remember, Mariette? It is a special day."

Mariette looked at me, shook her head. "I am sorry, Sylvie, but it needs to be said." She folded her arms, raised one perfect black brow, and said, "Paul, you are a generous and kind man, but it needs to be brought to your attention that this poor girl is in love with you...."

* * *

On the modern sea crossing to Arran, I finished my tea and waited to dock on the island. The rain held off, so I could stand outside and look at the water, watch the birds circling, imagine, as I always did, how things must have been centuries before.

Arran was one of my most beloved spots. Once a year or so, my mother and grandmother had gathered up a group of aunties and cousins and we all drove up to Ardrossan to take the ferry across. We'd picnic and tumble through the hills all day, then sleep overnight and come back in the morning. Glorious times.

It was my mother who'd shown Paul the cottage for sale in Lamlash, and he bought it nearly on the spot. It has other memories for me now, and I had not thought I'd like going across on the ferry this time, worried that the memory of that one piercing time would interfere with my pleasure in it.

To my surprise and pleasure, it did not. I stood on the decks of the ferry and watched the island approach, feeling something lighten in my heart. I remembered happy days with my mother, and Paul, and even my father, who'd sometimes come with us. Sunnier times than these.

As the ferry neared the bank, however, I felt nervousness well up in my chest. It had been a long time since I'd last seen Paul, and it seemed the last encounters had all been humiliating in one way or another.

The most humiliating was when he rescued me here, on Arran, when I was seventeen.

I did not think I would remember that one just now.

As I came off the ferry, I looked for him, my heart beating too quickly. I wondered if my face was red. And then I saw him and it didn't matter.

He stood against the gray sky like a pillar, in a long wool coat and a knitted scarf around his throat. He wore no hat, and his hair, a little long, very thick, blew in the wind. His face, long and carved, with harsh cheekbones and that strong Gallic nose, showed no expression.

And I could not help it—my heart squeezed so hard I almost could not breathe. What would I say, after all this time? What would he say?

As I came out of the gate, he spied me and came forward, rushing, I thought. Did I imagine that his expression brightened? I found myself hurrying, too. My heart hurt and I was determined not to show it. I thought I would faint with it when he stopped in front of me, and there was Paul, my Paul, standing there in the flesh after five full years. I could not find a single word to say.

But then he bent down and swept me up into a hug, his wool arms and gloves warm around me, and I flung my arms around his neck like a drowning child.

"Sylvie," he breathed against my ear. "Thank God."

For one long moment, I allowed myself to rest

against him, then I pushed a hand between us, and stepped back. I held up my hand, as if warding off an evil spell.

Something quivered in the air between us, a ghost, or the past, or a dream. Something. "Sylvie," he said, frowning, "you look exhausted."

"I don't have the diamond."

"Are you all right?"

"Luca stole it," I explained.

He lifted a hand toward me—I backed away. "How did you hurt your chin?"

"We need to go after him!" I said. "He's probably halfway to Romania by now."

"Sylvie—child—let me look at you! You have bruises!"

"Paul!" I backed away, out of his reach. "Are you listening to me?"

He caught my arms. "Are you?"

Something about the angle of his jaw, cleanly shaven, as if only moments ago, and a place on his exquisitely carved lower lip that was slightly chapped, abruptly unnerved me.

I suddenly *saw* him. A lock of thick, light brown hair blew across his brow. There was a thread of silver in it. I saw new creases at the edge of his eyes. His beautiful, beautiful gray-green eyes.

"I hear you," I said, deflating like a balloon.

He pulled off a glove and with his bare fingers

touched the marks on my face—my eyebrow and chin—and pressed his palm against my cheek, brushed hair away from my eyes. "Your lip looks very sore," he said, but did not quite touch it.

"I lost the diamond, Paul."

He nodded, shrugged. "We will get it back, do not worry. For now, Sylvie, come back with me to the cottage, and I will make phone calls, and make us a coffee. You look as though you could use it."

"All right."

He put his arm around me, in a bracing sort of way, and I melted all at once, just melted into the broadness of his chest and the smell of him, a richness I could never quite identify and was just…Paul.

At my capitulation, he enfolded me, resting his chin on top of my head, his ungloved hand cupping my ear, my face. I put my arms around his waist, closed my eyes. For this one minute, this one—

He bent his head close, pressed his lips against my temple. Fiercely, he said, "Sylvie, we must never let this much time go by again. Do you hear me?"

"Yes."

"Never," he repeated, and gave me a little shake. His lips moved against my brow. "I cannot bear it."

"I know. I'm sorry. You were right about him, about Timothy. I knew it that day."

"Shhh," he whispered. "It doesn't matter."

A wave of dizziness washed through me, equal

parts relief, regret, and love. Yes, it was still there, as solid as it ever had been. How could I have dared let so many days, weeks, months, *years* go by without hearing his voice, speaking his name?

"Paul," I said, just because I could.

"Sylvie," he said, and I felt him smile.

I needed to find out what part he'd played in all of this, what lines he had crossed himself. Squeezing his wrist to avoid showing my feelings, I slid out of his embrace. "Let's go then."

For a moment, he paused, *looking* at me. So intently. So closely. Then he nodded, held out a hand. "Come."

## Chapter 18

Cleavage: refers to the tendency of a diamond to split along the grain parallel to one of its octahedral faces. It is also a term applied to rough diamonds that have at some time been cleaved from a larger stone.

—www.costellos.com.au

Paul and I arrived at the cottage—and it really was a cottage, with whitewashed walls and a thatched roof that looked quaint and provided no end of headaches, not the least of which was finding a thatcher to do the upkeep. It was charming, however. Sometimes, violas grew in it, tiny purple and yellow flowers.

We arrived with the rain, which surged over the building like a wave blown up from the ocean.

"Good God," I said. "It's like Armageddon."

"Only Scotland," he said, and smiled. "You've just forgotten."

I held my hands out to the fire. A little nervous, maybe. Not looking at him too much.

He tossed his keys down and brought out a cell phone. "Forgive me," he said. "I must check messages."

"That's all right. Find out where Luca will be."

"I'm certain he's still in Scotland," Paul said, phone to his ear. "They've been canceling flights left and right all morning, thanks to weather. Gusts are too strong. He can't have gotten out." He picked up a pen and started writing on a tablet on the kitchen counter. For a moment, I watched him, thinking he looked like an ordinary businessman, in the long wool coat and the cleanliness of his hands. He looked like a television commercial for an upscale line of electronic equipment, or possibly wine.

Not at all like the Paul who had come here to rescue me when I was seventeen. Or maybe I was just old enough to finally see him clearly.

I had lived with my father for a year in San Francisco, but I did not fit in there, either. By then, I was fairly sure I didn't fit anywhere, and I would be a misfit in every school I ever attended. In America, I was lost in the popular culture everyone else shared.

They were joined together by sitcoms and commercials and a history of toys and books they'd shared—what did I know of *Wayne's World* or *Roseanne* or gangsta rap? I didn't understand American football or basketball and, having just come from Paris and Rio, hated the whole dressing-down idea for girls. What was the point?

They called me that "weird French girl."

With a crushing recognition, I realized it would be the same in Paris, perhaps even worse—there I would be the weird American, though perhaps my father's standing would have more clout in Europe. He was, in spite of everything, always in the top three drivers every year, and age seemed to be only giving him more power.

Actually, my father was fine, at last. We did have a lovely apartment in a good neighborhood, and I attended a good school. He, no doubt prompted by my grandmother and Paul, was attentive and learned how to spend time with a daughter. It helped that I was now a sophisticated sixteen-year-old instead of a gawky thirteen.

I was still painfully lonely. All through the rainy San Francisco winter, I pined for my Paris bedroom, the smell of Brigitte's cakes, the clatter of the produce vendors in the streets. And Paul, of course. To make myself less lonely, I immersed myself in the study of gems. It made me feel closer to Paul, but it was largely my own passion that made me want to explore them. I haunted the city's many museums, but there were not enough old or large gems to capture my attention, and I began to haunt estate sales.

In some ways, that was one of the finer times I spent with my father. Then, a happiness for him, a disaster for me—he fell in love. Not the lust-filled affairs he'd had until then. It was love, with a woman not quite a decade older than me. Clearly, she adored him, and it was mutual, and she was kind to me. But once they married, I decided it would be better to begin my own life.

Very maturely, I thought, I sat down with my father and asked his assistance. I wanted to go to Glasgow, to discover my Scottish ties, see who I was in that world. He agreed to give me a stipend and help arrange everything on two conditions: one, that I go into Ayr once a week and see my grandmother, and two, that I would choose a college and direction at the end of a year.

Fair enough.

So I established myself in a flat on the outskirts of Glasgow, and all I felt was lonely and lost. Bad months, those. I fell in with a fast crowd, drinking and other things, and I had my first lover, a boy two years my senior who had a nearly incomprehensible accent and a thick lock of hair that fell over his forehead in a way that slayed me.

But as first loves will, it ended, and badly. I caught

him with a pretty neighbor of mine, and that was that. In despair, I took the train to Ardrossan, called Paul to be sure I could use the cottage on Arran, and laid in supplies. Being seventeen and dramatic, it was in the back of my mind to commit suicide, and I suppose I wanted him to know where I was so when I didn't turn up they could find the body before it got too disgusting.

Instead, I fell asleep in the tiny bedroom, sobbing. I felt absolutely alone, deserted, crushed. It seemed there would never really be anyone in my corner, someone who had my back. I wished for a sister, my mother, even a single friend I could call upon.

Somewhere in that long night, I resolved to stop looking. I would be my own rescuer, do what I pleased and find my own way in the world. We were all alone, anyway.

When I awakened, there was a glaze of milky daylight beyond the windows, and standing before the kitchen windows with their starched eyelet curtains stood Paul in his shirt sleeves, cracking eggs into a blue bowl.

"*Bonjour, mon petit chou,*" he said cheerfully as I sat up. "Would you like eggs? I'm glad I thought to stop for supplies. There's not much here, and you look like a girl who could use a good cup of tea."

"How very British of you," I said, tossing my hair

out of my face. I tugged a sweater on my arms. "Yes, eggs, and yes, tea."

He smiled very slightly as I pushed by him to go to the toilet. I looked like hell in the mirror—swollen-eyed and splotchy—and of course, I'd forgotten a toothbrush, but he'd anticipated that and laid one still in its package on the sink. I tied my long hair back in a knot looped upon itself, and scrubbed my face with chilly water. It helped. I only looked a quarter dead instead of all the way there.

I went back to the main room, tugging on an oversized red sweater that I'd taken from a hook. It smelled of him. I lifted the sleeve to my nose without thinking, and only realized what I was doing when I saw him looking at me.

"You like that cologne?"

"I guess." I slumped the table and he put down a big ceramic mug of tea. "Thank you."

He kissed the top of my head. "You will live, no?"

"I didn't think so yesterday."

"So it is, with a broken heart."

"How did you know?" I straightened to let him put a plate of fluffy eggs and buttered bread down before me. He settled his own plate, discarded the apron, and sat down across from me.

"Eat," he said, nudging my hand.

I picked up my fork.

"I just knew," he said.

"I don't want to fall in love ever again," I said.

He nodded, and his eyes were kind. Knowing. Without a hint of irony, he said, "You will learn to bear it."

It was impossible not to remember it all, as I stood in the room where we'd spent so much time. It struck me that he was older. As I was.

I didn't actually know what he did for a living. Art collecting. Gems. He'd made a fair pile of money during his racing days and had invested wisely—but still. It often seemed there was a hushed aspect to his work. Was he a criminal? The aspects of Luca stealing the Katerina certainly seemed to suggest it.

I felt a sinking sensation in my gut, putting together these things I'd never thought about. When he flipped his phone closed and looked up at me, he must have seen it on my face. "I won't lie to you, Sylvie. Ask whatever you wish."

"Did you hire Luca to steal the Katerina?"

He stripped off his coat, folded it neatly over a chair, rolled up his sleeves. "Yes," he said at last. "It isn't quite that bare, but the short answer is yes, I did."

I sat on the edge of the sofa, my hands on my knees. "And you couldn't buy it why?"

His mouth turned up on the right. "I was trying to buy it. The dealer gave it to Gunnarsson for his debts."

With a scowl, I shook my head. "He had to have been a fool to throw away such wealth on a drug deal."

He simply lifted his eyebrows.

"Right. Drugs, fools, all the same." I rolled my eyes. "I still don't think it was okay for you to have it stolen."

He poured water into the kettle and set it to boil on the gas stove. "It isn't as if it was in a museum or some other sacred place. It wasn't even as if it had a proper owner who loved it had taken possession of it."

"Who appointed you judge of proper owners?"

He raised an eyebrow. "You know as well as I do that a jewel of such caliber deserves more than a casual or accidental owner."

Unconsciously, I touched the place where I'd been carrying the jewel and felt only the soft tissue of breast beneath fabric. I had to admit he was right. "I suppose so."

He took white cups off the shelf, and saucers and spoons, and set them on a bamboo tray. "Gunnarsson only wanted it to spite me. In such a circumstance, he deserved to have it stolen."

I rubbed my forehead. "I guess." With a sigh, I shook my head, spread my hands. "I don't know what the right answers are this time."

"How surprising," he returned, dryly.

I gave him a look. "At least I *try* to do the right thing."

"The implication there being that I do not?" It

made him angry. "Perhaps you are confusing me with your father."

"Don't start." The headache from last night edged back over my brow. "All I know is that I would not be sitting here if it were not for that jewel, that somehow I got mixed up in this mess because of my connection to you."

"That's true, Sylvie, but that involvement came from Colceriu, not me." He took a china canister from the shelf and flipped the heavy, rubberized lid open. The scent of coffee popped into the room. With a yellow spoon, Paul measured ground coffee into a French press. "I am not certain how he discovered your connection to me, but he used you to protect himself."

"I realize that, Paul." I scowled at him. "I'm not seventeen anymore. Or even—" I felt heat in my cheeks "—twenty-three. I can tell when a man is using me."

Mildly, he said, "Do not be so hard on yourself. Your ex-husband was quite practiced in his games."

"You tried to warn me. I didn't listen."

"We all have to make our own mistakes, *n'est-ce pas?*"

I lifted a shoulder. "Ancient history," I said. "I'm more concerned now with the current situation, and how convenient it all is. Luca tracked me down after stealing the jewel, and I just *happened* to be coming to Scotland for this case, which he—"

Paul lifted a finger. "I alerted the police to your reputation," he said. "When I heard of the other jewels the police seized, I knew they would bring in an assessor. I sent word of your credentials and your connection to the country."

"Why?"

"I wanted—" The kettle began to whistle and he grabbed a hot pad and lifted it off the burner, and poured it into the waiting glass pot. With a long wooden spoon, he stirred the grounds, put the lid on to brew, and only then looked at me. "I wanted to see you."

I met his gaze for a long moment, and again it was as if the ghosts were rising. I let them stand and dance between us and said only, "I see."

"Do you?" He shook his head. "I wonder."

If we started traveling this path, I simply would not be able to bear it. "We should focus on the jewel. How to get it back."

"Very well." He carried the tray into the living room area and settled it on a low wooden table. "First, a little coffee, hmm?"

Automatically, I shifted forward to serve. It made me think of the housekeeper who had taken such good care of me. "How is Brigitte?" I asked, picking up a cup and saucer.

"She is well. She retired last summer to go live

with her granddaughter in Castellane. The weather is milder there."

"Give her my regards." I poured coffee for him, dropped in a single lump of sugar, topped it with heavy cream. The tiny spoons I liked were in a neat cross on the tray and I settled one on the saucer before passing it to him.

He smiled.

"What?" I said.

"Nothing. I am only happy to see you, even if you are still angry with me."

"I am not angry with you."

"No?"

I shook my head. "I'm tired of anger. I gave it up for Lent."

His chuckle sounded as if it came from some deep place in his chest. "You've always been so very Catholic, haven't you, my little saint."

"Not lately," I said. And luckily, I had not been able to convince Timothy to get married in the church, or I'd be sitting here now in bigger spiritual trouble than I was already in. "Anyway, the jewel."

"What would you like to do, Sylvie? I am at your service."

I rolled my eyes. Before pouring my own cup of coffee, I shrugged out of my coat. The silk and linen blouse I'd taken from Luca's case was rumpled and wrinkled, but I still liked it.

Paul must have recognized it. "Was he your lover, then?" he asked.

I smiled like a Cheshire cat. "We should follow him to Romania," I said, pouring the rich, black coffee. "I think he will go first to his village, where there was a priest who used to sneer at him."

"What village?"

"That, I don't know." I stirred cream into my own cup. "I thought you might be able to find out."

He nodded. "Perhaps. What else?"

"There are some thugs, too. Or there were."

"The ones who were found dead?"

"Maybe." I frowned. "We startled one in my hotel room in Ayr, and then three at the caravan in Demure. Then….I know I saw someone on the road to Ardrossan. When I was talking to you on the phone."

"You should start at the beginning, Sylvie. How did you meet Colceriu in the first place?"

So I backtracked, filled him in on all that had happened since I got off the plane in Glasgow. I glanced at the clock on the wall and widened my eyes at the realization that it had barely been twenty-four hours since I'd landed. "Anyway, you said those men were reported dead, but I think someone else followed me. I also don't see how Luca could have killed them. They were big guys."

Paul lifted a shoulder. I noticed there were very fine pink lines in his pale gray shirt. "*You* got away."

"I broke one's knee, I think, and managed to get away from a second one, but nobody was dead when I left."

"I see." He straightened.

"So you didn't hire the thugs?" I asked.

A glitter lit those gray-green eyes. "Is that what you thought, Sylvie?"

"Maybe. Didn't seem to me that you'd just let him walk away with a jewel you've wanted since you were a child."

"And you would have been right. I had him followed by a thief, whom I thought would be able to steal it back, without much trouble." He smiled slightly. "I did not think it would be you he'd have to steal it from. Not until I had the message in voice mail."

Even in my current mood, I had to laugh at that. "So, that's who we surprised at the hotel?"

"Yes. Your grandmother told me where you were staying."

I nodded. It made sense. "But who are the others?"

"There were bound to be others who heard that Gunnarsson had taken possession of the Katerina. Competing drug lords. Petty criminals. They do no matter."

"I suppose not."

He pursed his lips, looked through the window, then back at me. "What do you wish to do, Sylvie? It is your reputation and it has become your quest."

"I called the inspector and told him I had it. My reputation depends on me delivering it now."

Paul nodded. "Do you wish to call him again and let him know it's missing?"

My nostrils flared. "No. Absolutely not."

"Then we go after Luca."

"Yes. That's why I'm here."

He inclined his head. "Is it?"

"Yes."

For a long moment, he only looked at me, a great quiet in his eyes, which were the color of a pool in a forest, something healing, something rich. Beautiful. That ache of longing, that had so much been a part of my emotions when I was with him, rose to full throated life.

Before he could see it, before it spilled out of my own eyes, onto my hot cheeks, I lowered my gaze, lifted my cup. "Yes," I said again.

"As you wish," he said, and stood up to make phone calls.

## Chapter 19

Diamond is distinctive in the way it reflects
light. It has a unique brilliance and also breaks
the light up into spectral colors, which reflect
within the stone as it is moved. Another unusual
quality of a diamond is it's purity. A gem quality
diamond is among the purest elements found in
nature.

—www.diamondgeezer.com

Paul called a friend who used the helicopter pad
based in Broderick, and they flew us to the Glasgow
airport in no time at all. At another time, I might have

enjoyed the experience, but all I could think about today was getting to Luca and the Katerina.

And maybe I was thinking about the jewel to avoid thinking too much about Paul.

It was midafternoon by the time we made it to Glasgow. Thin light edged the clouds, and splashes of daffodils, in medians and window boxes and flower pots, stood in brave testament to the coming of spring. It made my heart feel lighter.

At least until we passed the car rental counter on the way in. I spied the redheaded boy who'd asked about my father, "the greatest racer ever" and ducked my head in case he remembered me. I wondered where the red Alpha Romeo was now, if Luca had abandoned it here or somewhere else. And maybe it seems silly to you to feel bad about a car, but when I explained to Paul how I'd mistreated the lovely creature, he understood, rubbed one of my shoulders. We take cars seriously, we do.

Once we checked in, I felt the stares of other women on my grimy clothes and badly done hair and makeup. I didn't have a lot of time, but there were shops of all sorts. "I need to take care of a few things," I said to Paul.

"I'll go with you," he said. "It *is* clothes you're after?"

"Yes." I waved a disparaging hand at the makeshift wardrobe I'd assembled from my cousin's caravan, the old jumper and jeans over the blue silk shirt of Luca's. Still a fine piece, and I'd hold on to it.

Paul loved shopping, and although we did not have a lot of time, he took delight in pulling out a narrow, long black skirt and a body-skimming silk sweater with a low-cut V neck. While I tried them on, he tossed through a selection of scarves and pulled out three he liked—I wore the gossamer white one, tied around my throat.

When I went back to the changing room, Paul purchased other things for me, and had them tucked neatly into a carry-on bag I could put on my back. The supple leather felt like skin, and I exclaimed in pleasure when he handed it to me. "This way, you do not have to feel so deprived."

The clerk practically swooned over his continental manners, his accent, his handsome face. The Scots love the French, and vice versa, united as they are in their dislike of their common enemy, the English. As an outsider to all three, it seemed hilarious to me how nations carried grudges for so many centuries.

But there it was. We carried the packages to our gate area, and I left Paul sitting there while I found the ladies room and changed into the new clothes.

So much better! I folded the jeans and indigo silk blouse and tucked them into the plastic bag the other clothes had come in, then went out of the stall to examine myself in the mirror a little more.

My makeup was all right—I'd put some on before breakfast, then touched it up before getting off the ferry at Broderick before I saw Paul. The bruise on my chin was starting to show a little, and I put some more cover on it, pleased that it was going to heal very fast. A miracle I hadn't broken a tooth!

There wasn't a lot I could do about my hair, which was still caught in a long braid down my back. I knew from experience it was likely still damp, and that bugged me enough that I wanted to let it out. If you've ever had long hair, you know what I mean. After a while, you just need to let it go. Let it breathe.

I tugged the scrunchie from the bottom and worked my fingers through the braid. Wavy tendrils, some as damp as I'd anticipated, tumbled over my shoulders, down my back.

A little girl washing her hands in the sink next to me watched the whole process. Soberly, in an English accent, she asked, "Are you Rapunzel?"

Her mother chuckled. "Emma! Rapunzel is a fairly tale."

The girl looked unconvinced. "She looks just like the picture in the book."

The sweater was a romantic pinkish color, and the slim, stretchy skirt came down to my ankles, with a slit in the back. Together with the yards of blond, wavy hair, I knew what she was thinking.

I smiled at the mother in the mirror, and bent down to the little girl. "Well, I try not to let anyone know that I'm flying around," I said in a Scottish accent, "but yes, I *am* Rapunzel. Don't tell anyone, all right?"

"Oh, no," she exclaimed seriously. "I would never tell."

"Thank you," her mother said to me. "Come along, Emma. We'll be late for our plane."

The two went out, leaving me alone in the area by the sinks, and I leaned into the mirror to put on my lipstick. Fixed up, feeling a lot more cheerful, I grabbed my bag and headed back to the waiting area.

I saw Paul sitting there, spectacles low on his nose. He must need reading glasses! I thought with an odd pang. They were so endearing in some strange way I couldn't decipher just then, but it also broke my heart that he was older, that he would need such a thing. I hated it.

So I wasn't paying attention to anything but Paul when, abruptly, a hand grabbed me around the upper arm. The hand yanked me, so quickly I was knocked off balance, and stumbled in the direction they intended, into a dark cubbyhole, like a close between waiting areas. I tried to yank back, pull out, but he was stronger and threw me into the concrete wall, twisting my arm up behind me. I grunted, and his hand went over my mouth. I smelled onions on his fingers, and it nearly gagged me.

I twisted and jerked, trying to use his weight to get enough leverage to head-butt him, but he was ready or lucky, because my head met empty air. He shoved me again, and my body slammed hard into the concrete wall. A blast of pain from my bruised left breast went through me, and I gave a little yelp through the hand.

"Where is it?" he said, and lifted his hand for me to speak.

"I don't have it!"

He gripped me in a way that made it impossible to move, my arm swung up behind me and pressed into my back, my face against the wall. I could do nothing as he searched through the backpack, then very thoroughly patted me down, feeling breasts and crotch impersonally. It infuriated me, and I made a noise. "Stop it! I don't have it!"

"Where is it?"

"Luca has it," I said. "Somewhere in Romania."

The man made a sudden noise, something between a thunk and a groan, and the pressure of his body suddenly fell away. I pushed away from the wall, instinctively cradling my bruised chest. Paul took my hand.

"Come. Quickly," he said, and tugged me out of the dark spot.

I looked back over my shoulder, and the man was lying prone on the floor, his head at an odd angle. I pulled back. "God, Paul, is he *dead?*"

A pair of security guards were walking by and

Paul pulled me back into the opening of the little alleyway, blocking their view of the body. "Look at me, Sylvie," he said, turning my body toward his.

It was a dodge, I knew that, a way to keep the security guards from seeing the prone human on the floor, but it also slammed into me as a personal moment. The minute I raised my head, I knew I'd never forget this—the heat of him, the size of him, towering over me.

He pressed me into the wall and put his body close to mine. "Pretend you're kissing me," he said.

I met his eyes. It was a long, hot moment. I felt his body close to mine, knew he could feel the give of my breasts and belly against the length of him. His breath touched my lips, and I lifted my face the slightest bit, putting our lips only millimeters apart. "Like this?"

"Yes," he whispered back, and I could feel the heat of his mouth, the movements of his lips disturbing the air over my own. Against my thigh, I felt him grow aroused, and it was impossible not to move very slightly against him, acknowledging that arousal. His hand, on my side, edged upward over my rib cage, almost as if it were a being apart, and his thumb edged my breast.

Our lips still did not touch, but I could hear my breath coming a little faster. Infinitesimal movements pulsed through him, through me. A ripple of muscle in his left leg, a quiver in my belly, a nudge from his genitals, a pulse—known only to me—from my own.

"What excuse will you find this time?" I whispered.

"For what?"

"For turning away from me. I'm not a child anymore. I'm not going to be married."

"They were never excuses," he said

"No?" Boldly, I touched my tongue to his lower lip, very lightly, and the contact sent a bolt of sensation through my lower back so strong that I nearly felt as if I'd drop straight to the floor.

"Sylvie," he whispered, not moving. "Be careful."

"Yeah? You just want me to pretend? You don't really want me to kiss you?"

He raised his hand to the side of my face. "Look at me."

I raised my eyes. Every cell in my body boiled with a decade of wanting him. He caught my chin in his hand, held me still. Looking into my eyes, he imitated my movement, his tongue flashing over my lower lip. I made a sound, clutched his upper arm.

He did it again, this time more slowly, just a drag of the tip of his tongue along the round of my lip, a hot, measured gesture. "I have always tried to simply keep you safe," he said, and our eyes were locked, his greeny-gray, mine surely molten with my thoughts.

"And what," I whispered, my lips bumping his, "will you do now?"

"What do you want me to do, Sylvie? Hmmm?"

I closed my eyes. "I don't know."

"That has always been the trouble. You are not sure, and I will not risk losing you." His lips touched mine, very very lightly. "Once done," he said, "it cannot be undone."

"I know," I said, and hated the fear in my voice, the wavering. "Let me go."

He straightened. "Give me a moment."

At that, I smiled up at him. "At least it's gratifying to know that you do find me somewhat appealing."

"You could not have doubted that."

"Oh, but I have," I said. "Often."

He shook his head, took a breath, took my hand casually. "Do not doubt your allure, Sylvie."

"Thank you." We headed out into the main concourse, and they were calling for us to board Flight 329, with service to Munich and Bucharest. As we approached the area, he reached out and took my hand in his, not the grasp of a guardian to his ward, but that of a man to a woman. He didn't look at me, but I folded my hand around his in return, and held it until we had to go, single file, through the gate.

As we settled into the plane, the cabin was dimmed for takeoff, and Paul closed his eyes. I looked out the window, but it was the past I saw. Felt.

When I was seventeen, Paul had stayed with me for three days, cheering me up with little jokes and plenty of cheese and fruit and wine, which he'd never withheld and now said I was old enough to gauge if I wanted a second glass. I did, but not a third.

The last afternoon, we packed a picnic. Patches of heather were still black on the hills, but spreads of gorse were beginning to bloom, and here and there were scatters of daffodils, dizzyingly yellow against the dun and green of the land. On the top of a cliff, we spread out the picnic on a cloth and ate bacon rolls and potato scones, which made me think of my mother.

"Sometimes, I really miss her a lot," I said, gazing toward the water, blue against the rocks far below. "It doesn't seem fair, does it, that she got killed like that?"

"No, it does not."

I looked at him. Directly, I asked a question I'd held for a long time to myself. "Did you love her?"

"Of course I did."

"I mean *love* her, love her."

He met my gaze. "No. We were fine friends, but no more than that. She loved your father."

I jumped up, moving toward the edge of the land. The wind was blowing, and it made my eyes water, or so I told myself. I turned to find I was too close to the edge of a section of crumbling rock. A bit heaved, rumbled, something under my feet, and I screeched and leaped toward solid ground.

And as always, there was Paul, grabbing my hand, pulling me to safety. We tumbled to our knees, and I fell against his chest.

My heart pounded in reaction, and I lifted my head. "I'm sorry. That was stupid."

"It was," he agreed thunderously, gripping my hand too tightly. "You must stop being so heedless."

I don't know what made me do it. Maybe it was the daffodils, so yellow against the sky, or the feeling of his hand, or something hot and dangerous in his eye. I moved over him and put my hands on his face. I honestly do not think he had any idea what I was going to do until I did it.

Until I bent my head to his and kissed him.

I had been waiting all my life for that kiss, and the instant my lips touched his, it was as if the sky itself exploded, or maybe it was just me. His mouth was just…exactly right. His lips fit mine perfectly, and at first, that's all it was, just our lips touching, me draped halfway across him, his strong chest against my breasts, his cheeks in my hands.

"Sylvie!" He lifted me away from him, bodily, as if I were a pillow or a slight piece of lumber, instead of a tall, strong young woman.

I flung an arm around his neck. "Please don't push me away," I whispered. "I can't bear it."

"You are only lonely, my Sylvie. It will get better."

"No." I pressed closer, touched his face, his mouth, with my fingertips, and said, very seriously, "I have loved you all my life."

He made a low noise, protest and hunger mixed in

a heady brew, and instead of pushing me away, he relented, pulled me closer, tucked my head into the crook of his elbow. Our eyes met, electrically, and I had a sense of sunlight making a nimbus around his head, as if he were a saint, and a gust of wind touched our clothes. Under his breath, he swore, and then his free hand cupped my face and his lips came to mine, and he kissed me.

*Kissed* me.

His full lips claimed mine as if there were no other lips in the world, and behind that, his tongue swirling into my mouth, all the way in, and coaxing mine out, drawing me back into his mouth, then back across the tight bridge. He tilted his head, dove deeper, kissing me and kissing me and kissing me until I thought I would faint of love and pleasure.

I had been kissed many times. I had had my young lover.

But they had all been boys. Paul was a man. I'd never been kissed like this. It had never felt like this, so rich and right, as if everything aligned in the world with our touch, as if time itself shifted. I put my hands in his thick hair and pulled him closer, tighter arching upward against his body—

He pulled away violently, pushing me away. "Sylvie, we must not, this is—"

As if he could not bear the sight of me, he got to

his feet and strode away. I leapt to my feet. "That's not fair!" I shouted. "I am a *woman*. I love you!"

He whirled. "You are *not* a woman! You are a girl who wants to love someone, who wants someone to love her back."

"So? Isn't that what everyone wants?"

"Yes, but—"

Seeing my tears, he came close, put his hands on my arms, pulled me into his embrace. His hand in my hair pressed my face into his chest.

I clung to him, fighting tears.

"Oh, God, what have I done?" He clasped me close, murmured into my hair, "Oh, my sweet child, I am so very, very sorry." He pressed his cheek into my hair, a fierce and tender gesture that nearly liquefied me. "I am not rejecting you," he said. "It is only that you are the dearest thing in my life and I cannot bear to sully you this way. I am far too old to be your lover."

I started to move, push away, protest. He held me close. "No, Sylvie, listen to me closely. I will never say this again. I could not bear to see your eyes turn slowly to disgust as I grew older and older and older. You do not know what I know of the world. You must trust me."

"Paul—"

"No." His hand in my hair, his lips on my temple. "Promise you will forget this."

I squeezed my hands into fists, took a breath. How could I? But the alternative was to lose him, I could feel that very strongly. I let my tears well up again. "Will anyone ever love me, Paul? Will I ever be first?"

"Yes, *ma poulette*. There is a great love waiting for you, I promise. And—" he pulled away, turned my face up to his "—you are always my first concern. You are my heart. Always. Okay?"

I nodded. "Okay."

He let me go. "Come. Let's go find some vigorous thing to occupy us, and then, I think it's time we went back, don't you?"

## Chapter 20

The diamond is believed to make the wearer unhappy; its effects therefore are the same upon the mind as that of the sun upon the eye, for the latter rather dims than strengthens the sight. It indeed renders fearless, but there is nothing that contributes more to our safety than prudence and fear; therefore it is better to fear.

—Cardano ("Philosophi opera quaedam lectu digna," Basileae, 1585. "De gemmis.") from www.diamongeezer.com

What would have been different if I'd insisted, right then? It was impossible to know. Like the plane lifting off, leaving land behind, I left the memories behind in Scotland as we settled into our flying altitude.

I have always liked flying in the evening hours. The cabins are quieter, somehow more serene. Everyone has a blanket, a civilized pillow, a nice glass of wine with dinner—it was such a surprise to actually be served dinner that I was taken aback. "You don't get food on American planes anymore," I said.

"Not at all?"

"Well, I'm sure first class is served something on long flights, but no, not really."

"A shame, isn't it?"

Under the roar of the engines, he said, "Tell me about the Katerina, Sylvie. What was it like to hold her?"

I grinned at him. "Wickedly, wickedly wonderful."

"Yes?"

"Yes." I held up my hand, indicated the jewel's size on my palm. "She filled my palm, nearly, and the color is absolutely flawless, as if the purest water was frozen very quickly."

He listened intently, his nostrils flaring in hunger. "And the ruby? Is it really a pigeon's blood red?"

"It is, and it's almost a perfect teardrop." I raised a brow. "It really is one of the most beautiful jewels I've ever seen." I curled my hand into a fist and punched it into the other one. "That bastard! Dragged me into the whole mess, lets me fall in love with the damned thing, then takes off."

Paul narrowed his eyes. "Do you think he really wants to give it to the authorities in Romania?"

Without hesitation, I answered, "Yes. He wants to be a hero, like his father."

"And what, pray tell, did his father do?"

"He was a hero of some uprising, some valiant attempt to keep the Communists at bay or something. I don't know."

"Hmmm." Paul gave me a measured look. "You know a lot about him for such a short acquaintance."

"It's the war zone thing—close quarters, high stakes." I lifted a shoulder. "You talk."

"Is that so?" Casually, he sipped his scotch, put it down. "What will you do when you get the jewel back?"

I looked at him. "Take it to the Scottish authorities." I frowned, feeling the wrongness of that option. "Or not," I admitted. "I don't know. She kept leaping out of my hands—"

"Leaping?"

"Something. I dropped her three times."

He narrowed his eyes thoughtfully. "It is a very cursed stone."

"I know." I put my palms together, remembering the vivid vibrational qualities. "It's also a very powerful stone. It should have gone to a sorcerer."

That amused him. "The Sorcerer's Stone?"

"Yeah." I laid my head back against the seat and yawned. "I'm tired now. I'm going to sleep for a while."

"All right."

I closed my eyes and leaned against the wall, feeling the cold through the metal.

Next to me, Paul raised the armrest dividing our seats, and pushed his tray into the upright position. "Come," he said, and patted his chest. "Rest here."

For a moment, I hesitated, then slid forward and nuzzled in to the hollow just below his shoulder. His arm, big and comforting, fell around me, a protection. I closed my eyes, feeling his breath move in and out, in and out. I heard the tinkle of ice in his glass when he lifted it and swallowed.

When I was a child, his was the lap I was most likely to choose to sleep in. I'd crawl up and put my head on his shoulder, as now, and go instantly, immediately to sleep. He would hum under his breath, stroke my hair, rub my toes or my wrists, and I'd sail away to dreamland, protected and comforted.

Two decades had gone by, and it had not changed. His voice started to rumble out of his chest, very low, almost subvocal, some lost French folk tune from his childhood that he always sings under his breath.

A thousand phrases passed through my mind. Why have you never married? What do you really do for a living? Have you ever seen me as a woman? Will you ever?

But the past forty-eight hours had been very

intense, and my body's need for sleep was higher than my mind's need for answers.

When I awakened, the lights in the cabin were dimmed, and apart from the white noise of the engines, there was hardly any sound. For a moment, I was disoriented, knowing it was a plane, that I'd fallen asleep. I could hear a low rumbling of two Scottish voices a few rows behind me. I couldn't make out the words, just the rolling lilt of the rhythm, the song of their accent.

Last was my realization that I'd fallen asleep on Paul's shoulder, and he'd fallen asleep, too. He snored, very lightly, over my head. It made me smile.

As gently and slowly as possible, I disengaged from his heavy arm, and he stirred, resettled, but didn't open his eyes.

It gave me a chance to just look at him. The high-bridged nose and exquisitely cut mouth, the thick, wavy hair. His hands were long and graceful, and I wanted to put my lips to the hollow of his throat.

What had he said to me that day on the cliff in Arran? That he would not be able to bear seeing me grow disgusted with his aging.

I looked at him seriously, constrasting him with the young, vigorous Luca. Paul was not a young man anymore. I didn't know exactly how old he was, but he'd been racing some years when my father met him, and he had to have been in his late twenties at that point. He was younger than my father, but not very much.

And it wasn't as if he were aging like a movie star. Here and there, the sleek waves of his hair showed threads of glittery silver. The temples would be quite silver before much longer. In the skin around his eyes were weathered lines from laughing, and the marks of time in a thousand tiny places on his face, neck, hands.

I felt around inside my chest for revulsion over those signs of age and felt none. Each thing was only Paul, dear because it belonged to him.

My feelings for him had never shifted, never changed. I loved him. I wanted him.

A hollow feeling invaded my upper stomach. He had almost been lost to me this last time—my own snit—and I couldn't bear to have another misunderstanding. I'd flung myself at him just before my wedding, and he had resisted, refusing to either be my excuse for ending the ruse that was my wedding, or relenting enough to give his blessing. He'd only said that Timothy was using me, and put me away from him quite firmly.

Terrible scene. And I should have had the courage to walk away from the impending wedding, but I didn't.

Paul shifted beside me, his hand reaching for mine even in sleep. Suddenly, my wish to possess him seemed madness, the madness of youth, a petulant desire to have everything my own way. I turned away, stared out the dark window, seeking signs of life. I spied a string of little villages, likely scattered down the length of a river, and a road or two. In the distance was a city of some size, shining white across a bend on the horizon. I wondered what it was.

The world was so huge. In every one of the villages were particular lives, with mothers and fathers, weddings and births and love affairs, tragedies and dramas. Each little village. Each neighborhood in that white city.

And what difference did my story, my loves, my drama make?

Paul stirred next to me. I didn't turn, afraid my dark thoughts, my insecurity and indecision, would show on my face. His fingers moved against my palm, and I allowed it, clinging to the sturdy broadness. He was the single steadiest thing in my life. I would not risk it.

I looked over at him. Our eyes met, and he lifted my hand to his lips.

We did not speak, only traveled the rest of the way in quiet.

## Chapter 21

Until the 15th century only kings wore
diamonds as a symbol of strength, courage and
invincibility. Over the centuries, however, the
diamond acquired its unique status as the
ultimate gift of love. Indeed it was said that
Cupid's arrows were tipped with diamonds
which have a magic that nothing else can ever
quite equal. Since the very beginning, diamonds
have been associated with romance and legend.
                              —www.costellos.com.au

Bucharest was freezing cold, and a heavy, wet snow
was falling. As we headed for a cab, I shivered into

my coat. "I haven't had the right clothes on this entire trip," I said. "I need jeans and a down vest."

"We'll be going into the mountains in the morning," Paul said, and gestured for me to get into the cab ahead of him. "There is no point going tonight, so we'll have some supper, and in the morning find you something to wear that's warmer. I've arranged for a car to be delivered to the hotel."

"You made reservations already?"

He gave me a slight smile. "Of course, my dear. One would not want you left out in the cold."

"I see." The cab was warm and my body relaxed a little. "Have you ever been here?"

"No."

"Do you know where we're going to try to find Luca?"

"He's from a village in Moldavia. The weather has been stormy the past few days, so with any luck, he's not made it home yet. We'll hope to reach it first."

I nodded.

"Do you know," he asked, folding his glove-clad hands in his lap, "what you'd like to do, once you have the jewel?"

"There's really only one answer—I have to call the Scottish police and let them know. I already left a message on the voice mail of the inspector who gave me this job."

"I see."

"Are you going to be angry with me?"

He looked at me. "No." He lifted a shoulder. "Disappointed."

I narrowed my eyes. "Oh, don't do that. Don't give me that disappointed thing."

"Would you rather I lied to you?"

"I don't know. No. Yes." I scowled. "No. But don't make me feel lousy for doing what I think is right."

"I am not the one who is concerned." He cleared his throat. "What if I am the first to get to him? What if I take possession of it? Will you feel required to tell the police where it is?"

"That's not fair."

"But why not? I have been working a long time to find the Katerina. I very nearly succeeded in possessing her, and now she slips through my fingers at the very last moment?"

"I don't want you to have her," I said, my chin jutting out.

"Why not?"

"The curse! You should see Luca. He looks awful, and he's nearly been killed three times since he stole the jewel."

"Come now, Sylvie, you don't really believe in the curse?"

"I don't know. I told you there is a very strong feeling to her. I don't know that the stone itself is malevolent, but there is definitely a lot of negative emotion attached. I don't want you to be hurt or killed."

"What about you? You've been injured since she was in your possession, too. How will you avoid the curse yourself?"

"I don't know. Maybe I won't. Maybe it will be like some dark fairy tale. Rapunzel lets down her hair and the dragon eats her anyway."

Gruffly, he said, "Do not say such things."

I looked out the window. It was too dark to make out much of the city itself, but I saw nineteenth-century buildings mixed in some weird way with Stalinesque abominations, and very modern office sorts of buildings. The indelible gray finger of communism is hard to erase. "Then don't ask me to imagine a fate like that for you."

He was silent for a moment. "Do you know the legend?" he asked.

"Yes. A prince brought it to his bride. She was murdered. He killed himself. It was buried with her, and then some priest ordered it to be dug up. Forever after, it brought bad luck and death."

"Only partly correct."

I looked at him. "What is the rest?"

"It is said that true love will break the curse. That one who loves truly, giving it to the object of that affection, will end it."

"Oh, please." I rolled my eyes. "There's no such thing as true love."

"Tsk, tsk," he said with a low chuckle. "You believe in the curse, but not true love?"

I shrugged.

"So young to be so cynical."

"Can you blame me?" I looked out the window. "My mother, my father, you, my own marriage—it's not exactly as if I've seen anything close to true love in my life."

"How me? What did I do?"

"You have never married. You've never seemed to ever be in love with anyone. You go along almost pathologically unattached."

His laughter was rich and merry. "Is that so?"

"Yes!" He started to add more, and I raised a hand. "Don't, okay? I'm not in the mood."

"True love does exists, *ma petite puce*."

"Whatever." We were halted at a traffic light, and we listened to the engine rumble for a long moment. Then I said, "Didn't the prince love the princess truly? He gave her an awfully big jewel."

"He stole her from her true love. He lusted for her, did not love."

"Isn't it always the way."

We pulled smoothly into the rounded drive of a tall, stone fronted hotel. Women in evening gowns that swirled out from beneath heavy coats were escorted by men in tuxedos. "It looks like a ball," I said. "How appropriate."

Paul laughed.

If I hadn't been watching the skittering trail of a shiny blue dress, I would never have noticed the blue stripe on the pant leg of the man next to her, which led me to noticing another man next to him.

It was the man from the airport in Glasgow, the first time. The big redheaded thug who'd shown up in Dunure.

"What the hell?" I said aloud, peering at him, sure I was mistaken.

But no. He looked sturdy and elegant in a tuxedo and cummerbund, had his arm on the elbow of a woman in a apricot-colored gown. A white bandage covered a wound on his right hand. Probably where I'd bitten him.

Without a second's hesitation, I leaped out of the car.

He spied me when I was only a few feet away, and took off, running full tilt through the crowds, knocking people aside. "Wait!" I cried. "Let me just talk to you!"

But of course, he didn't. I chased him into the ornate lobby of the hotel, and through a doorway. I dashed behind him, bumping into a woman, then a man, apologizing, ducking their frowns. When I ran through the doors, I found myself in a sea of tuxedoed men. A waltz was playing and mirrors reflected the whole dazzling satin and silk display. I stopped, flummoxed.

It seemed as if there were thousands and thousands of men in tuxes. For a few minutes, I pushed through, hoping to get lucky, but I knew it was hopeless. I returned to the lobby, where I spied Paul, looking frustrated and upset as I came closer.

He grabbed my arm. "Do not do that to me again, do you hear me?"

There was genuine fury, perhaps worry, in his tone. "I saw—"

"I don't care." He tucked my hand through the crook in his elbow, and held it there. "Tell me upstairs. Now, let's check in."

We checked in as Mr. Paul and Ms. Diamond, which Paul thought very funny.

"Oh, yes, Mr. Paul," the man said in heavily accented English, "and you have a package for your daughter, which will be delivered to your room shortly."

"Very good."

I was stung by the "daughter" comment. "That wasn't very politic, was it?" I commented quietly as the bellboy led us to the elevator. "What if he'd just called your wife your daughter?"

"It's a suite, with two bedrooms," he said.

"Oh."

Within the elevator, with mirrors reflecting us, Paul so elegant, me so much younger, looking very much as if we were father and daughter, I felt tangled and irritable and nervous. I said nothing until we were shown into the suite, an expansive set of rooms with views looking over the sparkling lights of the city.

"Why are we doing this?" I asked. "Shouldn't we be headed to the mountains?"

"It is snowing in the mountains, Sylvie. No one is driving there tonight." He looked around the room, poked his head into the bedrooms, nodded in satisfaction. "Thank you," he said, and tipped the boy. He departed, and when the door had closed, Paul tucked his wallet back inside his coat. "I have a plan, believe it or not. Perhaps you should trust me."

I paced to the window, peered out at the city, at a roundabout where little-toy-looking cars whirled around, brake lights flashing in the snow. "Maybe I would if you shared the plan with me."

"Ah, here we go," he said as someone knocked. "Here is part of it, Sylvie, if you want to stop sulking."

I turned as he opened the door. A man carried a garment bag and a box with what were presumably shoes. Paul spoke to him quickly, reiterating something, and the man nodded. A young man with a white jacket, he bent and smiled in my direction. Paul closed the door. "I told him it was your birthday and he is going to bring champagne."

"How will that help us get the jewel?"

Paul carried the bag to a door, where he hung it up. "We must go downstairs to the ball." He flipped the bag away from the clothing below and exposed a black dress with a low neckline and a low back. A wrap was draped over the hanger. "I had to guess the sizes, so I hope they are all right. Here are shoes—" He raised them. "I will leave you to get dressed. A half hour?"

"It's beautiful," I said honestly. "You always have great taste, but I don't understand. Why are we going down there?"

"I suspect your friend Luca may be there tonight."

"Why? You don't think he's on his way to his mother's village?"

He didn't look at me immediately, instead smoothed a hand over the skirt of the dress. I liked the look of his big hand, so male and square, in contrast to the delicate material of the dress. "Perhaps," he said, finally. "But perhaps it is more likely that he knew of this gathering some time ago and knew he could use the jewel to curry favor."

I blinked. "So the village story was just to get my sympathy."

He shrugged.

"God, I'm an idiot, aren't I?"

"Not at all, Sylvie. He is afraid of the jewel, and he wanted to get it here. At any rate, there are any number of jewel aficionados in the gathering downstairs, and some others who may be of help to us. It was no accident I booked this room, this hotel and I arranged for the dress from Scotland."

"All right. It won't take me long to get ready." I kicked off my shoes and strode across the room to take the dress off the door. "You don't have to go anywhere. I'll be quick."

He stood where he was, looking down at me. "Are you nervous, Sylvie?"

"No."

"I think you are." He touched my chin with one finger. "I suspect that you are worried that you have set things in motion that you do not know if you wish to ride forward—you should forgive the double entendre." His smile was wry, his eyes so clear and sage.

I swallowed. "I don't know."

"It is all forgotten."

A sense of pressure drained out of me suddenly, replaced almost as quickly with regret. Push. Pull. My heart pounded. "I'll get dressed," I said, and took the dress into the bathroom.

I hung it on a hook and smoothed my hands over it. Exquisite, as would be any dress of his choosing. I stripped off my blouse, skirt and bra. The sudden fall of support reminded me of the bruise, and I turned to look at myself in the big hotel mirror.

"Jeez," I said aloud. The lower half of my left breast was a deep purply blue, and the red mark in the middle perfectly imitated the ruby at the heart of the Katerina.

But that was not—not by a long shot—the only bruise or mark on my body. There was a trail of little marks down my thigh, a bruise on my elbow, a scrape on my knee I didn't remember getting, and of course, the bruised chin.

No help for it. I put the dress on over my head, and it slid silkily into place over my skin. The neckline was plunging, showing nice plump rounds of breast on either side—I would have to pin it to hide the bruise on the left—and a cut that left nearly my entire back bare, all the way to the base of my spine. With long, close-fitting sleeves, the exposed skin was elegant rather than slutty, and I loved the swirl of the skirt over my hips.

"Nice," I said, admiring the back. I slid into the high-heeled sandals and headed out to the other room for my bag, where I had some lipstick and mascara to touch up my face.

Paul was opening a bottle of champagne when I walked out, and he stopped to admire me properly. "That looks very, very nice, Sylvie. I knew it would suit you."

I spun around, feeling a heady sort of recklessness as air swooped over my bare back, as the skirt swirled around my legs. "It's beautifully cut," I said.

He poured champagne into two glasses for us, and handed me one. "To a successful venture this evening," he said. "Cheers, *ma poulette.*"

I grinned at his endearment. "Cheers." We clinked glasses and each sipped. Then I remembered the revealing nature of the neckline. "I think I need a safety pin, though. Let me check for one, so you can see if it shows."

"A pin? For what? I don't see the need for a pin."

Unthinking, I touched the edge of my left breast, and pushed a little fabric aside. "I have a pretty bad bruise."

"Sylvie!" he exclaimed, and put his glass aside. "Have you had someone look at it?"

"No—when would I have had time?" I raised an eyebrow. "You're welcome to the job."

"Christ." He stepped forward, lifted a hand, put it back down. "What did you do to yourself?"

"I was carrying the Katerina in my bra, and had a little fall." I touched the bruise on my chin, too. "It happened all at the same time."

"Well," he said, "pin it, I suppose, for tonight. We'll find someone to look at it later."

Some evil part of me wanted to poke at him, protect myself. "Not you?"

"That's enough," he said, mouth grim.

Stung, I turned away, put the champagne down, and absurdly found I was blinking away tears. It felt, suddenly, like the awful night when I was sixteen and Mariette's deliberate humiliation of me. "Fuck you," I said before I realized I would.

In two strides, he was across the room, capturing

me from behind with an arm looped around my neck. He pulled me against him, kissed my hair.

"Sylvie, Sylvie, Sylvie. You cannot know how many arguments I have had with myself over you." He touched the side of my neck with his fingers, brushing downward, softly, erotically. "How often I voiced both sides of the argument. One day, I say to myself, you are a woman, finally grown. The next minute, I see some tenderness, some delicate thing about your collarbone that makes me think you are still so young, so vulnerable."

Tears burned in my eyes. "Not that young."

His mouth touched my neck, lightly, with full heat. "I do long for you, my Sylvie. It is that love that keeps me from it." The last was said fiercely. "Do you hear me?"

My hands were shaking, almost violently. My own conflict, made plain. I leaned back into him, feeling the fabric of his shirt against my naked back. "Yes. I hear you." Taking a breath, I straightened. "But what if the reason I haven't been able to find a soul mate is because I already found one?"

He didn't speak. Only pressed his mouth to my shoulder.

"What if you are my soul mate, Paul?"

He touched his nose into my neck. "Let's go find your Luca and get your jewel to safety, then we will deal with each other, hmm?"

*I am a fool,* I thought to myself. A foolish girl with foolish passions and confused motives. Hadn't I been lusting over Luca only hours before, wanting *his* hands, *his* kiss? And on the way to Scotland, hadn't I been nursing the humiliation of my divorce?

Was I so pathetic I just wanted someone to love me for a day, or a night?

Was that so bad? To long for the loving touch of a man, his arms around me? I'd gained strength from having Luca hold me last night.

But it would be an entirely different thing with Paul. It would be an irrevocable act with long-term consequences, and I wasn't sure whether I was more afraid to discover that I genuinely loved him, or that I didn't.

I had lost everyone I loved, one way or another. It would be too hard to lose Paul.

"You're right," I said, and stepped away from him, mustering a smile I hoped looked a little more genuine. "Let's do it.'

The ball was a birthday party for a lovely young woman with hair piled onto her head. Next to me, Paul said, "She is descended from the former royal family. I think her brother will know where we shall find Luca."

"Good."

We moved through the crowd, smiling, nodding. My hair was piled on my head, little waves left free to tickle my shoulders. The dress drew no small amount of attention, and I was pleased to recognize Paul was sticking close to me because of it. His hand strayed to the bared small of my back, lit on the center, swept the nape. It aroused me and annoyed me and pleased me all at once. "Who are we looking for? Luca?"

"Luca, mainly, but who was it you saw earlier? The Scot?"

"Yes, he was one of the thugs."

"Would you recognize any of the others?"

"Maybe. I don't know. It was dark. I knew him because I saw him earlier, at the airport." I frowned. "I'm concerned about this, about who might be chasing us. There had to be two groups, right? Yours, and the ones who got killed."

"Yes."

I scanned the crowd carefully. "So who hired the big Scot? The one who is here tonight?"

"I don't know. Someone else obviously knows the jewel is tremendously valuable."

"Right."

"We need to be very alert. Don't go too far from me. We should be ready to give chase or get away very quickly if need be."

"Why would we need to get out quickly?"

"He might try to run when he sees me, no?" He shifted his shoulders restlessly. "There is trouble brewing. I've got the Jaguar ready, too." He patted a pocket. "It is parked to the front—turn right and it's just around the corner."

"Black, I assume?"

He smiled. "Of course."

"Did my father have a hand in that?"

"I don't need your father, Sylvie." He grinned down at me. "You're forgetting who *I* am."

I raised my brows. "That's an interesting question, Mr. Maigny. Who are you, anyway? Are you a criminal?"

His gaze traveled around the edges of the room. "Not really. Perhaps, in some small ways. Mostly, I have invested in real estate." He smiled down at me. "Not quite as exciting."

"Real estate?" I echoed.

"Yes. As it happens, I own quite a lot in California and London, and in other places I think will be good investments over time."

"Hmm." A little something in me eased. "That's better."

He laughed softly. "Too much imagination, *mon petit chou*."

Too easy. "Oh, no you don't," I said. "You dabble in jewels and painting and the thieves who might find them for you."

"Do I?"

"How else—" Something caught my attention out

of the corner of my eye. "Never mind. Look to your extreme right. I believe we have our mark."

It was Luca.

## Chapter 22

In some cultures there is still a deep superstition about diamonds. For example, in the Malaysian diamond mines if a stone contains in its center a gray or black ghost diamond, the well where it was found is abandoned: a Malaysian legend holds that these stones hold the "soul of the diamond", and the mine will die if its soul leaves it. However, diamond soul is a personal talisman that people will wear as an amulet.

—www.diamondgeezer.com

Luca stood there in a tuxedo with a blue satin cummerbund, his hair falling in those gorgeous curls around a face that was pale and marked by our journey.

"Ah."

Luca did not appear to feel nervous or worried—he gave every appearance of a man having a lovely time at a party. He smiled at the woman, who was dark and rosy-cheeked, like Snow White. With a sense of determination, I moved forward.

Paul caught my arm. I shook it off with a glare. "Let me handle this," I said.

Maybe it was something in my expression, or perhaps he finally understood that I was not the vulnerable child he'd once had to rescue, but he let me go. "As you wish."

I made my way through the milling people, edging along the wide, polished floor where couples danced a waltz. They made me think of a jewelry box my grandmother had, with tiny spinning couples on a floor of mirrors.

As I edged closer, Luca, perhaps alerted by the odd sense of being watched, looked around the room, still talking to the young woman in front of him. When he caught sight of me, his face shifted, alternately dismayed and pleased. I almost could see him formulating lies to tell me. To my surprise, however, he didn't bolt.

Luca kept his eyes on me as I approached, and I realized that the young woman he spoke with had a similar look to the birthday girl. She was likely a royal, too. Luca's cousin.

What had he said? Fifth in line for the throne?

From a waiter carrying fluted glasses of champagne, I snared a drink, and approached the pair. "Luca!" I said with a French accent. "How lovely to see you!" I turned to the girl, holding out my hand. "Hello. I am Sylvie Montague. My father is—"

"Yes, I know you," the girl said in Dracula-accented English. "Your photos are in the tabloids all the time." She managed to get a sneer into it, as if it was my fault, the act of an ill-bred sort.

I tossed my head back and laughed gaily, as if it were such a funny joke. Taking Luca's arm, I cozied up to him, pressed my breast into his upper arm. "You must have seen the ones of us kissing in Scotland, then, hmm? It was the whim of moment, and now all the world thinks we are lovers."

Her tight smile said she'd not seen those particular photos, and she was not pleased. "How vulgar."

"Oooh," I said, "I am so sorry! Did I misunderstand?"

Luca said smoothly, "This is Anya, Princess Anya, actually." He met my eyes. "My cousin."

"What a delight to meet you!" I cried, and without letting Luca go, lifted my glass her way. "Since he is your cousin, it is all right that I have been feeling my heart flutter about him since I first saw him at the airport."

"Of course. I cannot think of any reason I would mind." She raised her haughty chin. "Excuse me."

Luca said something in Romanian, obviously an attempt to smooth things over. She flashed him a furious glance over her shoulder.

"Sylvie, I beg you," he said, turning back to me. "Do not do this thing. My moment of triumph is at hand. The entire royal family is here. They want·this jewel. There are some who believe it will restore the throne."

"Well, bully for them." I edged him closer to the wall. "The trouble is, Paul paid you for it, so it technically belongs to him."

"No. Technically, it belongs to me until I return it to the crown jewels with which it belongs." His eyes blazed. "Beyond his reach."

"Luca," I said in a weary voice, "one way or another, I'm leaving here with it. If you just give it to me, I'll walk away. If you hold on to it, you'll go to prison in the UK for theft."

He laughed.

"Where is it?"

He gave me an amused glance. "It is quite safe."

"Mmm." Over his shoulder, I saw Paul not far away, and made eye contact, gave him a slight nod. "The thing I wonder, Luca, is how you feel at all safe, with thugs all around, and me, and Paul Maigny, all on your tail."

"Surely you have guessed by now?"

"What?"

"That 'thug' you chased earlier is my bodyguard, Sylvie."

A series of events snapped into place—every time I'd seen him, Luca had been nearby. I struggled not to let the revelation show but Luca laughed contemptuously.

"You are in over your head. Go home, go back to Scotland, and let the big boys play with the real rarities."

"Don't bother my pretty little head? Is that it?"

"Exactly."

Paul had come up from behind. "What about mine?" he said, and, touched Luca's shoulder.

Luca didn't wait—he bolted, straight for the door to the back of the room. I made a dive for him, and caught his sleeve for a moment, but he tore away, fast as a running back, and was swallowed by the crowd. Hobbled as I was by the high heels, Paul blasted by me, shoved keys in my hands. "Go," he cried. "Get the car and bring it to the back of the hotel."

I spun around and ran in the other direction, headed for the front doors, and the Jag.

It was snowing outside and I had nothing but high heels and a skimpy wrap to protect me from the cold. Spying a man's brown overcoat on the counter, I snagged it on my way by, ignoring a howl of protest from behind me.

Outside, I paused for one second to get my

bearings and shove my arms into the coat. It was far too big for me, but the hem dropped well below my knees, and it was very warm.

The sidewalk was slippery, but I had learned a long time ago how to run in even the highest heels—it was a matter of balance and strong ankles—and I managed to stay upright. Skittering around the corner, I saw the Jag, unmistakable in its shape, even when covered by the snow. I opened the right side—saw that I was again in a right-hand drive country—and dashed around to the left. Dizzying, this business of driving on different sides, with shifting equipment.

Since I'd learned to drive in France and the U.S., I was happier on the right hand, and although there was always the slightly disorienting moments of shifting back to the default mode, it didn't suck to drive a Jaguar. Ever. "Hello, darlin'," I said aloud, gleefully listening to the engine rumbling to life.

We all have our favorites. The Alpha Romeo was a lovely creature, responsive and sleek, but if given a choice, I always loved a Jag.

I kicked off the high heels and jumped out to wipe snow from the back window with my sleeve, fast as I could. I didn't even know where the back of the hotel was—it had seemed as if they were going that direction.

The question was answered when Paul yanked open the driver's side door and said, "Let's go! Move!"

In most cases, I would drive, but he was the

Formula One champ, not I. Not matter how great a driver I was, I could not come close to him, and I dashed to the passenger side.

"What's going on?"

"He's got a driver and a car. I don't know who it is, but we'll stick with them."

"I know who it is," I said, jumping in. "I kept thinking he was a thug, but he was with Luca all along. Luca's bodyguard."

A dark sedan tore out of the alley behind the hotel and sailed around us, going the opposite way. I saw the driver, and of course it was the redheaded thug I'd first seen at the Glasgow airport, the one I'd bitten at the caravan. "Get in," I cried. "Come on!"

"Sylvie, I came to this side by mistake. You have to drive."

"You're the champ, not me."

"I cannot drive like you can, not anymore. Not since my accident."

Startled for one long second, I thought of him lying in that hospital bed in Nice for so very long. He'd never gone back to racing, but it had never occurred to me it was because he *couldn't*.

"Ah, I hate that look on your face," he said.

As I stood by the car, a voice sailed into the night. "Hey, princess!" said a skinny man smoking a cigarette. "What brought you to Bucharest? This your new boyfriend?"

Before I even processed it was the *effing* papa-razzi, he'd snapped a series of pictures—me in the stolen oversize coat and bare feet, the Jaguar with open door, Paul, looking so very, very Continental. Depending on our expressions, this could be good for almost anything.

I collected my scattered thoughts and dashed around the car in my bare feet. "Get in," I cried. "Let's go for a drive!"

He grinned and dove in the car. We buckled in, and I threw the Jag into gear. Luca and Frankenstein were ahead, but I wasn't particularly worried about it. No contest between a Jag and a sedan, no matter what the make. I punched the accelerator and pulled out, crossing three lanes of traffic to slip the nose of the car neatly ahead of a taxi who leaned on his horn without restraint.

Traffic was heavy—perhaps dinner traffic? "What day is it?"

"Saturday."

"My time-space continuum is really distorted."

Paul laughed. "It happens."

"I need to remember," I said, watching a motorcy-cle roar between two lines of cars to snake up behind us, "that my father is racing tomorrow."

"I'll remember. Kuala Lampur, is it?"

"Yes." The photographer from the hotel was on the motorcycle, with someone on the back. They'd obviously abandoned the hopes of seeing royalty for a photo op of a different sort. "Damn them!" I said. "We don't need this headache along with everything else."

"Ignore them."

The other trouble was, there were dozens of dark sedans in the congested street as we approached a roundabout. I thought I spied the car and pushed across the lanes only to discover it wasn't Luca at all. The motorcycle came right behind us, in no hurry.

"There is your prince," Paul said, pointing to the left. "Go!"

The light had turned and traffic was pouring like water through the intersection. The car, a dark blue Audi, with the distinctive five circles and a European Union circle on the bumper, swirled into the roundabout, edging to the left. I followed, trying to beat back a sense of urgency.

"There he goes!" I cried and accelerated, shoving through thick lines of cars with fury as the Audi broke out of the roundabout and headed down a side street.

Traffic was less congested here, but the Audi wove in and out, dashing through little breaks, headed down alleyways and through side streets in a way that let me know the driver knew the city well. Behind us, shooting photos in a lazy way, were the photographer and his pal on the motorcycle.

Snow was still falling, and there were horns

honking and the streets were slick. "Frankenstein knows how to drive," I said aloud.

"He's taking us somewhere," Paul said. "This is too easy."

"Well, then," I said, shifting and pressing down on the accelerator, "let's take the lead then, shall we?"

I zoomed through traffic, the Jag smooth as a knife through butter, and the sedan speeded up, looped through a residential area, and dashed through a small park. "What are you doing?" I murmured.

Around me, the Jaguar seemed to come alive. The faster we went, the better the engine purred, and I thought of my father, racing around the tracks of the world, around Monaco and Kuala Lampur and all the other exotic places he raced through my lifetime.

He loved it, and he'd given it to me, the only thing he really had.

Frankenstein suddenly cornered around a tight, almost geometrically triangular turn and accelerated wildly as he drove down a deserted, dark street. I glanced in the rearview mirror to see the motorcyclist was still with us.

Speed was very high for these conditions, the heavy snow, the slick roads, the twisting, turning back streets—

The road swerved suddenly to the left, a brutally sharp angle that ran along a body of water. "Shit, shit, shit, shit!" I cried, downshifting, holding my breath as I tried to keep the Jag from spinning out entirely on the curve. We slammed over a low curb, narrowly missed a tree, skimmed along the water for fifty yards, and managed to get back on the road.

The motorcyclist, too, was still in the running, and the trio of us went sailing over a bridge, past a giant white Stalin-era building, back into a dark road, and along a very long park.

"This is getting old," I said.

"There's a wide area coming up. See it?"

It was a square of some sort, maybe the center of a park. I slammed my foot down and raced forward. Just ahead, the dark sedan picked up speed to attempt to stay ahead, and just as I felt the first nerve-wracking loss of traction an instant before I lost control, I saw the Audi hit a patch of ice and start to slide.

At the same instant, the Jag skidded into the same ice and whirled like a top, spinning so hard it was like a merry-go-round.

"Hold on!" I cried.

"Keep your head low!" Paul yelled, and just then, the motorcycle slammed into us, the machine crashing into the windshield, the humans somewhere else. In the blindness, I couldn't see where we were going.

"Paul!" I cried.

"Hang on, hold on. You can do it."

I clung to the shivering steering wheel, and suddenly, it was as if I *became* the car—I was no longer skin and limbs and brain, but suddenly melded with the car. I could feel the tires as part of my body, feel where they met the road, feel the engine rumbling through my lungs, my belly. In my groin was the center of balance, and my hands were the wheel.

It was still a struggle to regain control, to steer against the spin and avoid braking, which would only slam us even further out of control. The car slowed, and slowed, and I raised my head to steer us to a stop—

And heard a huge, slamming explosion.

I knew that sound.

For an instant, I waited for my body to break apart, go spraying out into the ether, but nothing happened.

When the car spun out, my body—and Paul, I noticed—had gone into an instinctive crouch, intensified when he'd yelled at me to duck, and now I straightened.

"Are you all right?" I asked.

"Yes. Are you?"

"Fine. Who crashed?"

"I think it was the Audi," he said grimly.

The Jaguar was running. I shut it off. It was amazingly quiet.

We opened the doors to a scene of carnage, made all the more unnerving by the absolute silence that accompanied it. The motorcycle was mangled, on its side, front wheel spinning crazily. I saw one person lying in the road, another sitting up. I hoped the camera was lost in the water at the very least. Bastard.

"Stay here, Sylvie," Paul said. In his voice, I heard the horror of what he was seeing. I glanced over, ready to look away fast, but I needed to know what exactly had happened.

The Audi had slammed into the side of a bridge. There wasn't much left of it.

My tolerance for car wrecks is miniscule, given the nature of my father's profession, the number of gruesome deaths I'd seen over the years. This was a bad one. I turned away, retching, and then realized that Paul was going to search Luca's body for the Katerina. In the distance, sirens started whooping.

"Paul, don't touch it!" I cried, and dashed toward him. "Please!"

He stopped me with a hand held out, fingers pointing in my direction. "Come no closer," he said. "You will not want this scene in your imagination, *ma cherie*."

His expression was so severe, I halted. "Please don't pick it up."

"Close your eyes, Sylvie, and turn around."

I did as I was told. Snow lit on my face in little splotches, and there was a smell of gasoline and hot antifreeze dripping on engines, and the ticking of cooling metal. I thought of Luca on the road in Scotland, and pulling him out of the wrecked car.

"Hey, princess," said the photographer. "Smile, baby."

My eyes popped open and I saw the photographer

lift his camera and shoot the wreckage. Something in me snapped, and I roared across the space between us, snatched his camera, and threw it will all my might into the lake. "People died here, you bastard!"

He smiled. "Yep. And I've got it all right here." He showed me a small digital camera, and then sprinted into the night.

I let him go, the will to follow drained out of me by the long, long hours I'd been running, chasing, ducking. Bastards. It was a sick way to make a living.

The sirens were whooping closer and anxiety sprang up in me. I didn't turn around. "Paul, we need to go."

He came up beside me. "One moment, Sylvie," he said.

I looked at him. His expression was deeply serious, his eyes grave. In his hand, he held something. It was covered with blood, blood that also covered his hand. I hated the symbolism, the grimness of that vision. "Paul—"

He held up one finger from his other hand, then went to the edge of the lake and knelt, dipping the Katerina into the water, bringing his hand and the diamond up clean. He walked back, stopped in front of me, and soberly, ritualistically, raised his hand and opened his fingers, so the Katerina, clean and gleaming, dripping with water from the lake of her own country, sat like a plump egg in offering.

"She is yours, Sylvie Montague."

I stared at him, remembering his words in the car. If I took it and gave it back to him, perhaps the curse would be broken. If my love was true—

I bowed my head, plucked the jewel out of his hand, and tucked it in my pocket. "Let's go."

He took my hand, and we walked into the night, leaving the carnage behind.

# Chapter 23

The very word "diamond" comes from the Greek "adamas" meaning unconquerable, suggesting the eternity of love. The Greeks also believed the fire in the diamond reflected the constant flame of love. For millions around the world that fire, the mystery and magic, the beauty and romance shining out from a simple solitaire says all that the heart feels but words can't express. However, it wasn't until 1477, when Archduke Maximilian of Austria gave a diamond ring to Mary of Burgundy, that the tradition of diamond engagement rings was born.

—www.costellos.com.au

We returned to the hotel and slipped in the back way. Impossibly, the ball was still going on, the laughter louder, the pleasure cranked up a notch. We went upstairs without speaking.

I was exhausted, sick at heart, confused.

And aching to be held. I thought of all the years, all the many, many, many nights I'd lain in a lonely bed and thought of Paul. Not many men, men who sometimes took his place, the *one* man.

This one. Paul.

We entered the suite and Paul locked the door, put out the Do Not Disturb sign. "We should sleep in tomorrow, hmm?"

"Sure."

My body buzzed with a dizzying mix of exhaustion and electricity and anticipation as I took off the drab brown overcoat, then reached into the pocket and pulled out the Katerina. I put it down on the table and we both reverently bent over it.

"Magnificent," Paul said.

"You know that I would give her to you if she were mine to give."

"Yes."

"Do you think it was the curse that killed him?" I asked quietly.

"I don't believe in curses," Paul said, and looked at me.

"I didn't think I did, either, but there's no denying

that people who get mixed up with this jewel often die gruesome deaths."

He cocked his head, and a smiling light edged into his irises. "That's like saying cocaine is a curse, isn't it? It isn't the drug, it's the activities surrounding it that cause destruction."

"Right." At his proximity, at the closeness of his sage-green eyes, I felt suddenly dizzy, and straightened, putting cold fingers to my forehead. "Whew."

"Are you all right, Sylvie?"

"Would you mind doing me a favor?"

"Of course."

I turned around and lifted my hair from the back of my neck. "Would you kiss the top of my back, just there? Just once or twice?" I pointed to a place at my nape. "There?"

He didn't move immediately.

"Please?" I said quietly, firmly.

His sleeve rustled as he moved, and the air was disturbed around us and his lips touched the back of my neck. His lips, then his tongue, drawing a little circle there. "Like that?"

"Again," I said and my voice was barely a whisper.

He slid an arm around my waist, and I bowed my head, my hands still holding my hair out of the way. He kissed each rise of my spine, lips first, then tongue, then moved and did it again. "What else?"

"My ear," I whispered, and he obliged me.

"And here?" he asked, kissing along my shoulder.

"Oh, yes."

My hands started their trembling again, and my knees were a little unsteady too. I let it fill me up, the hunger, the fear, the conflict between wanting him and being afraid to ruin everything.

I turned. "I have never, in all my life, wanted someone to kiss me as much as I want you to kiss me now," I said, and put my arms around his neck. "Can you forget everything else and just kiss me?"

"I cannot forget," he said, and his voice was gruff. "I have waited a thousand years for this, Sylvie. A million." His breathing was unsteady, and he cupped my face, lifted my chin with his thumbs, and kissed me.

Kissed me.

You think you know what a kiss is, how it proceeds, but this was not like anything I'd ever known before. The opening of his mouth, the thrust of his tongue, the way I opened to him, to take him, all of him, into my mouth. I wanted to swallow him, or crawl into his mouth. I couldn't breathe with the wanting, with the fierce thrusting need to inhale him. I stumbled forward, pulled him tighter, pressed my body against his.

His hands were in my hair, on my neck, and I shoved his coat from his shoulders, kicked off my shoes, started pulling at his shirt. It felt I would die of the need to see his chest, bare, with hair across it; die of the contact I finally made with it. I broke free of his kiss and pressed my nose into the very center of his rib cage, breathed in the concentrated essence of his skin.

I opened my mouth and tasted his skin.

*Paul's* skin.

I wanted to weep with it, and I lifted my face to his again, and there were tears on his face, falling on me. "Oh, God, oh, God," I whispered as he kissed me, pushed the dress from my shoulders, down my arms, baring my breasts, which I pressed into the silky hair on his chest, belly to belly, chest to breasts, my skin and his, and our lips tangling, his tongue so deep in my mouth, and then drawing me deeply into his. He made a soft, harsh noise as the dress fell away to my waist, and picked me up, pulled my groin into his; I wrapped my arms hard around his neck, my legs around his waist, and kissed him even more, even deeper, breathing in, tasting, touching, feeling—

It seemed impossible. Impossible. Wonderful.

This was Paul, *my* Paul. Whom I had loved all my life. Whom I had wanted for at least a decade, probably longer. Finally kissing me, me kissing him, as we were meant to do. His hand in my hair, drinking of my mouth as if he might die without it, his arm around my waist, an urgency about us that was dark and thrumming with unsaid, unsayable things, expressing a thousand moments of loss, of connection, of longing.

He put me on the bed and paused, over me, looking at me, touching my face. So seriously, so soberly, with so much awareness it pierced me through. He kissed me, slowly, breathing my name between the press of our lips—*Sylvie, Sylvie, Sylvie. My love, my love*—his hands pushing away my hair, exploring my shoulders.

I touched him, running my open palms down his back, surprised by the tensile strength there, corded below his shoulder blades, down his spine. I reached below his belt, in his trousers, to touch his buttocks, pulled him closer to me.

His arms were trembling, and I felt that echo in my whole body, too. "Take off my dress," I said, gasping. "Take off your pants."

"Yes," he said, and scrambled up, tugged my dress the rest of the way off me, leaving me in ordinary bikini panties. I lifted my hips and skimmed them off, too. I lay there, on a hotel bed in Romania, at last naked before Paul Maigny, the man I had seen at seven and turned to my mother and said, "He is the most handsome man in all the world and I am going to marry him."

And that man, still lean, still more beautiful than anyone I'd ever known, looked at me, stricken, his big, raw-boned hands loose at his sides. "Oh, my Sylvie, you are wounded because of my greed."

I sat up, reached for his belt, kissed his belly urgently as I worked the buckle loose, bit at his navel, rushed to skim away his trousers before he let himself be lost in musts and shoulds and all those other things that would come between us much faster than I would like.

And then, he, too, was naked, and very aroused, and I raised my face and smiled. "Oh, you are splendid, my love. Even here, you are splendid." I kissed him, his member, and he pushed me, climbed onto me on the bed, put our bodies, finally naked, together. He kissed me, deeply, slowly. "I cannot bear to rush, Sylvie. Forever and ever I have wanted to touch you this way. I have thought of it a thousand times."

"A million," I whispered, cupping his face in my hands, wrapping myself around him, feeling him rock and slide against me. Naked chests, bare arms, nude legs, unclothed, undressed. At last.

At last.

He kissed me, and we pressed together as if we could sink into each other, trade cells, meld entirely. I struggled to stay conscious of the now, of this moment, this moment when at last I could let free my passion for this particular man, touch his skin, kiss his mouth, put my hands in his thick and wavy hair. "Oh, Paul," I whispered. "Paul."

At last we could no more contain the hunger, and

he moved me, parted my legs and looked at me, and then guided himself in, into the warmth. He filled me, slowly, slowly, slowly, and then paused there, braced himself on his elbows and said, "Look at me, Sylvie. Look at me."

"I see you," I whispered, and it was true. I stared right into his gray-green eyes, saw the flicker and wounds of his life; he moved, slowly, slowly, kissed me again, looked at me, and we both had tears on our faces, and we fell into the depth and pattern of our own creating, something that seemed it had been waiting for me all of my life. As my orgasm built, split me, as he slammed into me, his legs sliding against my thighs, his hands hard in my hair, his tongue deep in my mouth, I heard a catch in his voice, and he came, his mouth on my throat, my chin, my face, my lips. "Sylvie," he choked. "Sylvie. Sylvie."

We lay together in the quiet, curled under blankets while the snow muffled all external noises. We touched each other in that longing, wordless way— our fingers lacing together, then coming apart, my body pressed into his, my leg over his thigh.

I wanted to say, *I could live here, in this moment.* I wanted to say, *I have never loved anyone in my life the way I love you.* I wanted to spill my heart, my guts, my soul to the one man who might really understand me.

But what if he didn't?

He kissed my forehead, my crown. "Sylvie, do not think too much, love. Let it be."

I nodded against him, but what did that even mean? Let it be. I slid my hands through the hair on his chest. "Your skin is so silky," I said.

"Mmm. So is yours."

He slid downward. Kissed my neck. Gently bent over my bruised breast and kissed it. Spread a hand over my lower belly. I put my hands in his hair and drew him upward to me, and kissed him. "What does that mean, Paul, not to think too much? Do you love me?"

"Yes," he whispered. "But I am not going to hold you back from the things you deserve. Children, stability, a man who will not go to his grave decades before you."

"Don't say that!" The idea of him ever going to his grave brought tears of loss, a searing kind of fear into my heart. I couldn't bear to think of it.

"I have spent years trying to keep this from happening," he said, brushing hair over my face. "I thought we might finally be safe when you married. I had hoped I was wrong about him."

"Well, you were right."

He braced himself on his elbow, looked down at me. His hand, huge and encompassing, curled around my cheekbone and jaw. "And don't you know, in your heart, Sylvie, that I am right about this, too?"

"No," I said. "I think you don't believe in me enough."

"I believe in you now. But I have also walked roads that are yet in front of you, and there are things—" he shook his head "—that will challenge you."

"And you're afraid that I'll betray you or something? Is that it?"

"No, no." He bent close, covered my mouth with his, and we got lost in kissing for a moment. "Quite the opposite—I fear you would discover you do not love an old man anymore, and you will suffer along without leaving me, longing for someone else."

"Paul!" I cried, aggrieved. "You don't believe that?"

"You don't know what life can do to a person, Sylvie."

I pushed my face into his shoulder. "Stop it."

He moved his hands over my back, down the hollow of my spine to my buttocks. Kissed my shoulder. "Whatever happens, Sylvie, I want you to remember one thing."

I looked up at him. "What?"

He swallowed, rubbed his thumb over my forehead, along the edge of my eye. "I love you."

It frightened me, the way he said it. Why did it suddenly feel that I was going to lose everything, just when I'd finally found it?

# Chapter 24

In Hindu mythology, diamond has a great importance. It is the vajra (lightning, the weapon of Indra, main god of the Hindus), and by the six points of the octaedra symbolises the true man who resists to attacks from the north, south, east and west, from the infernal powers and celestial powers. Therefore a diamond bearer is protected from fire, poison, thieves, water, snakes and evil spirits.

—www.diamondgeezer.com

When I awakened, Paul was not beside me. I sat up straight, blinking, and called out his name, listening in case he was in the shower or something.

Only silence greeted me.

I hate it when people leave me sleeping. It no doubt loops back to my mother, and I ought to get over it, but my fear of abandonment is quite strong.

Which Paul knows. It was a trauma even when we were in Nice, long ago. He would not leave me like this. Not while I slept.

Unless he took the Katerina.

With a cynical smile, I stood up and padded across the room naked. The Katerina was still there, as bright as if she was a star, or a lightbulb. She glowed, as if she had some internal source of light.

Next to her was a gray envelope with my name written on it in Paul's continental hand. My heart sunk.

It was hard to read the note at first, because my tears blurred the page. If I'd been looking for the truth of my feelings, I suppose I had them now.

He'd written in English:

My dearest Sylvie,
    I know you will be angry with me for leaving you as you slept, but I do it to protect you. This morning, you will look into your heart and you will know what you feel for the world, for yourself. You've made it through your divorce.

You have accomplished a major coup by capturing this lost gem. You are beautiful, and brave, and sensual and smart. There is not a woman on this earth who is your equal. You are a tiger, burning bright. The world is yours, my sweet.

The one thing I would ask is that you not let our one digression affect what has been the source of my strength for many, many years. Without you, I am lost. Without me, you have no champion.

I am ever your servant,

Paul

PS I think her name now is Katerina's Heart, don't you?

I picked her up. She was still a very powerful stone, but now it seemed there was a radiance to her, a beauty that had been washed clean of greed and unholy desires.

And it suddenly occurred to me where it should go. What I should do. Lifting the beautiful, storied gem to my lips, I kissed her and said, "Now that I've brought you home, I must ask a petition."

As if she heard me, the spirit of the stone, it felt like it was buzzing in my hands. I pictured the life I wanted, with my love, the one I had longed for all these years. "I will take you to your rightful place," I said aloud. "In return, let me go to mine."

For a long time, we sat in the quiet, Katerina and I, and then I looked at the clock and saw that it was nearly ten.

My father's race! In a rush, I ran to the television and started flipping channels. Surely someone carried the race!

The sound of engines alerted me to the right channel, and I sat down in my robe, the remote control in one hand, the Katerina nestled in my other. The cars were lined up, and the camera panned over my father's, a sleek yellow beauty he called—what else?—Sylvie.

"Go, Dad!" I whispered. And bit my lip for an hour until the race was done.

Gordon Montague, oldest Formula One driver in the world, won.

# Chapter 25

April 7, 20—
FAMOUS GEM SURFACES
BUCHAREST (AP)—One of the world's most valuable diamonds, thought lost for decades, surfaced in Romania yesterday. An orthodox priest received a letter giving directions to a grave thought to contain the original remains of a 13th century princess, Katerina Colceriu, whose brutal murder was thought to kick off a centuries-long curse attached to the stone that bears her name, Katerina's Blood.

The diamond, more than 80 carats, was wrapped in a lock of blond hair that had been braided and tied around it, and it was tucked inside a small pouch. Although police searched for clues to the identity of the deliverer, no answers were expected.

A note within requested that the name of the diamond be changed to Katerina's Heart.

The airport is the same grimy Jetsonesque place it always is, but nothing can dampen my excitement at being back in France. As I climb out of a cab in the Marais district, the air smells of blossoms and chocolate.

The florist on the corner has giant masses of daffodils, and I ask her to wrap up a huge armful, which I carry in my arms with a bottle of wine up the stairs. The building smells of onions and I can hear the old woman in the courtyard humming an old French love song.

I knock on the door, and there's grumbling with, *"Un moment!"* then the door swings open and Paul gapes at me. His sleeves are rolled up on his arms, and he's had his hands in his hair, and he looks tired.

*"Bonjour, monsieur."*

He still just looks at me.

I can see I am going to have to do everything. "You know," I say, "there are no guarantees. Maybe you'll meet a dashing beauty who steals you away from me. Maybe I'll fall in love with a gardener. My career is very busy and so is yours, but—can we try to be lovers? Just for a while?"

He steps forward, puts his hands on my face. Speech seems beyond him.

With a little smile, I hand him the flowers. "Would you please kiss me?"

He flings an arm around my neck, bends down and kisses my throat. "Oh, my Sylvie, I have missed you so very much."

"I know," I say, and the world shifts. Sylvie the seven-year-old and Sylvie the twelve-year-old and Sylvie the twenty-eight-year-old, all sigh together as he lifts his head, bends over our lips and gives us all a lovely, long kiss.

"Hey, what's this?" says a voice that startles and thrills me. I pull away from Paul to see my father, hale and tanned, standing in the apartment living room.

With a laugh, I rush forward and give him a hug. "Now you show up, after all the adventures!"

His strong arms practically crack my ribs, and he laughs his big, hearty laugh. He's not reliable, my father, but he's wonderful, and his life has made him the kind of man to whom I can say, "Hey, Dad. I want to introduce you to my new boyfriend."

For a moment, they measure each other, Paul and my father.

Then my father nods. "Nice to meet you."

We all have supper on the Rue de Sévigné, and drink wine, and it's exactly all that I could ask of the world.

At least for now.

*There's more Silhouette Bombshell coming your way!*
*Every month we've got four fresh, unique,*
*satisfying reads that will keep you riveted.*
*Turn the page for an exclusive excerpt*
*from one of next month's releases*
*SURVIVAL INSTINCT*
*By Doranna Durgin*
*On sale April 2006 at your favorite retail outlet.*

Karin paused at the basement's side door, hefting the hand cultivator. She stuffed the worn leather gloves in her front jeans pocket and the trowel in her back pocket, and she glanced back at Dave Hunter. Assessing him.

She needed him to wait, but she also wanted the backup if things went badly. She wasn't sure if he'd do either.

He stood awkwardly in the filtered light, more awkwardly than she would have thought possible just from watching him move—the movement of a man who was fit, who knew himself and knew what he could do. But she didn't need him barging into the discussion, not when she still had a chance to chase these fellows off without too much fuss.

Not a very big chance. But still a chance.

He shifted his weight back and Karin nodded to herself. He'd wait. In the end, he'd do what everyone did—serve their own best interests. These men had come after her because of *him*. No doubt he didn't really want to be caught out.

She didn't give him time for comment or question. She turned away, hesitating just long enough to swipe her fingers along the dirty windowsill and smear it across her cheek. She tugged a few strands of hair loose from her low ponytail and adjusted her T-shirt.

When she walked out the door, it was with the air of distraction. A woman at work, thinking about garden frost dates and soil preparation and just how many zucchini would that one plant produce, anyway? She walked uphill toward the porch steps, still hidden from the men by the back corner of the house—but only until they stopped lurking on the wrap-around, ready to expand the search. They moved heavily down those concrete porch steps; they had none of Dave Hunter's lightness of foot.

Too much bulky muscle.

They hadn't spotted her. Not yet. She was too close to the house, too peripheral. But any second now...

She took a deep breath. God, they were big. And though she knew how to take care of herself, she was no superheroine. She talked her way out of trouble, or flirted her way out. She depended on those skills.

And there. Now they spotted her. They stopped at the bottom of the steps and she slipped into the role. She started backward, raising a hand to the base of her throat as her sister, Ellen, had often done when confounded. "I didn't know—" She pressed her lips together as Ellen might have done, too, stopping her uncertain flow of words. "Can I help you? Are you lost?"

The two exchanged glances. On eye level, they turned out to be a Frick and Frack pairing—one swarthy, with wavy black hair slicked back in... geeze, was that some updated version of a mullet? The gangster mullet. Great. The other fellow had the look of an ex-boxer, nose and ears damaged, his hair cut in a dull brown crewcut. It made his head look like a pasty football.

*Do not underestimate the pasty football.*

They made their tacit decision—yes, she was the right one—and the mullet-haired one said, "Barret wants to talk to you."

*Oh, does he?* But that's not what Ellen would say, and if she'd learned one thing, it was to preserve her cover at all times. "I'm sorry...I don't think I know—"

The ex-boxer snorted. "He said you wouldn't want to come."

"Look," she said carefully, Ellen's body language

in place. "I was in an accident. There's a lot I don't remember. I don't know who Barret is." And dammit, she didn't. Another one of those things Ellen hadn't mentioned.

"You were in an accident." The swarthy man's words were as flat as his gangster mullet.

"Doesn't matter," said the other, both to his partner and to Karin. "Barret wants to talk to you. So let's go. He said you could take the time to pack a bag. Something pretty, he said." He looked her up and down, gaze hesitating at her artful smudge of dirt and then again where the breeze caressed her exposed stomach, and his lip lifted slightly. "Let's go."

She couldn't even begin to pretend that the rising goose bumps were a byproduct of that breeze. These men weren't here to talk. They were to fetch her to Barret, and they were already bored.

"I can't go," she said, hunting strategy, finding nothing. "Not right now." Damn, these guys looked bigger every moment. *C'mon brain, think!*

Except Barret Whoeverhewas sounded like a man who was used to getting what he wanted. Hell, if he had these two on his payroll, he probably *was* used to getting what he wanted. No matter how outrageous it would seem to Mr. and Mrs. Middle-Class America.

Karin wasn't Miss Middle Class. She had, in fact, been raised as Miss Snake-in-the-Gutter. But she knew how to buy time. "I can't go," she repeated, a little louder. Just to make sure Dave Hunter knew exactly what was going on here. *Just be ready,* she'd told him. If Ellen's memories really mattered to him, he'd try to protect them—and by default, her. She gestured with the cultivator. "I've got planting to do. I can't miss the season. And the goat is ready to drop her kid." She cocked her head, pretending she didn't see the subtle annoyance in Frick and Frack, or the impending escalation of the situation. *Saint Arthelais, this potential kidnap victim would use a little help here.* "Can't he just call me? Or he's welcome to come here—"

The ex-boxer rolled his eyes. "Not gonna happen."

Dave Hunter had done this, had led these Neanderthals into her life. Too ironic, considering what she was really hiding from. *Oh, Ellen, why didn't you warn me?*

As if she'd had the time.

Karin struggled to contain her resentment, channeling it into Ellen's wary fear. Not hard to do. "I'm sorry," she said, lifting her chin slightly in a gesture opposite to her own habit of dropping her head to look up from beneath her brow. "I can't do that. I don't know you and I don't know your boss and I want you to leave now." If Dave Hunter didn't take *this* hint, he was deaf and dumb—most particularly, dumb.

Or maybe he just cherished his own safety more than he needed Ellen's memories.

"Let's go," the ex-boxer said, but he spoke to his

companion, jerking his head toward their car. "We're wasting time. She can pick up some things when she gets there."

*Run, Karin, run.* Surely they wouldn't have her stamina. And they'd never find her once she hit the woods—

Karin blinked down at her biceps, suddenly engulfed in the ex-boxer's grip. Not so slow after all. And it *hurt,* dammit.

Ellen's persona went away. Karin snarled—her own voice, her own words. "I said *no!*" She tightened her fingers around the cultivator as she jerked against his grip, feinting toward the obvious target with her knee. Boy, did he look smug as he straightened his arm, pushing her out of reach and leaning forward a little to do it.

Not so smug as she whipped the cultivator up and buried it into the side of his face.

# SURVIVAL INSTINCT

## by Doranna Durgin

Former bad-girl Karin Sommers had distanced herself from her con-game past by assuming the identity of her deceased sister. But her sister had witnessed a terrible crime, and the perpetrators were dead set on covering their tracks. Soon Karin was back on the run... from someone else's past.

*Available April 2006
wherever books are sold.*

If you enjoyed what you just read,
then we've got an offer you can't resist!

# Take 2 bestselling
# love stories FREE!
# Plus get a FREE surprise gift!

**Clip this page and mail it to Silhouette Reader Service®**

| IN U.S.A. | IN CANADA |
|---|---|
| 3010 Walden Ave. | P.O. Box 609 |
| P.O. Box 1867 | Fort Erie, Ontario |
| Buffalo, N.Y. 14240-1867 | L2A 5X3 |

**YES!** Please send me 2 free Silhouette Bombshell™ novels and my free surprise gift. After receiving them, if I don't wish to receive any more, I can return the shipping statement marked cancel. If I don't cancel, I will receive 4 brand-new novels every month, before they're available in stores! In the U.S.A., bill me at the bargain price of $4.69 plus 25¢ shipping & handling per book and applicable sales tax, if any*. In Canada, bill me at the bargain price of $5.24 plus 25¢ shipping & handling per book and applicable taxes**. That's the complete price and a savings of 10% off the cover prices—what a great deal! I understand that accepting the 2 free books and gift places me under no obligation ever to buy any books. I can always return a shipment and cancel at any time. Even if I never buy another book from Silhouettte, the 2 free books and gift are mine to keep forever.

200 HDN D34H
300 HDN D34J

Name _____ (PLEASE PRINT)

Address _____ Apt.# _____

City _____ State/Prov. _____ Zip/Postal Code _____

*Not valid to current Silhouette Bombshell™ subscribers.*

*Want to try another series?*
*Call 1-800-873-8635 or visit www.morefreebooks.com.*

\* Terms and prices subject to change without notice. Sales tax applicable in N.Y.
\*\* Canadian residents will be charged applicable provincial taxes and GST.
  All orders subject to approval. Offer limited to one per household.
  ® and ™ are registered trademarks owned and used by the trademark owner and
  or its licensee.

BOMB04                                      ©2004 Harlequin Enterprises Limited

## USA TODAY
## BESTSELLING AUTHOR

# Shirl HENKE

### BRINGS YOU

# SNEAK AND RESCUE

## March 2006

Rescuing a brainwashed rich kid
from the Space Quest TV show
convention should have been a cinch
for retrieval specialist Sam Ballanger.
But when gun-toting thugs gave chase,
Sam found herself on the run with a truly
motley crew, including the spaced-out
teen, her flustered husband and one
very suspicious Elvis impersonator....

Signature Select™

*She had the ideal life...*
*until she had to start all over again.*

**National bestselling author**

# VICKI HINZE

*Her Perfect Life*

**Don't miss this breakout novel!**

---

## $1.⁰⁰ OFF

your purchase of
*Her Perfect Life* by Vicki Hinze

5 65373 00076 2   (8100) 0 11209

---

www.eHarlequin.com

HARLEQUIN®
*Live the emotion*™

©2006 Harlequin Enterprises Ltd

Signature Select™

*She had the ideal life…*
*until she had to start all over again.*

**National bestselling author**

# VICKI HINZE

*Her Perfect Life*

**Don't miss this breakout novel!**

www.eHarlequin.com

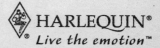
HARLEQUIN®
*Live the emotion*™

©2006 Harlequin Enterprises Ltd

## Silhouette®
# BOMBSHELL™
## COMING NEXT MONTH

### #85 SURVIVAL INSTINCT by Doranna Durgin
Now living in peace on a Blue Ridge farm, former bad girl Karin Sommers had escaped her con-game past by assuming the identity of her deceased sister—until Karin discovered her new identity came with serious baggage. For her sister had witnessed a terrible crime, and the perpetrators, fooled by the sibling switch, were keen on offing Karin to cover their tracks. Soon she was back on the run...from someone else's past.

### #86 FLASHBACK by Justine Davis
*Athena Force*
The women of Athena Academy looked out for their own. So when new information surfaced about the decade-old murder of academy founder Senator Marion Gracelyn, FBI forensic scientist Alex Forsythe took the case in a heartbeat. With the help of fellow Athenas and FBI agent Justin Cohen, Alex pursued leads to the power corridors of Washington, D.C. Was it just a hunch—or was there a killer hiding out in high office?

### #87 RUN FOR THE MONEY by Stephanie Feagan
CPA Whitney "Pink" Pearl felt noble working for the Chinese Earthquake Relief Fund—until she discovered someone was embezzling from the charity in her name. She was even framed for a coworker's murder! Never a quitter, she went on an intercontinental mission to prove her innocence, with Russian mobsters in hot pursuit. But it was her romantic pursuers—an attorney and a U.S. senator—who really had Pink blushing.

### #88 MISSING INCORPORATED by Tess Pendergrass
Travel reporter Magdalena "Mad Max" Riley more than earned her nickname as a moonlighter finding missing persons. So when her media-mogul client turned up dead and his twelve-year-old son ran away to uncover why, Mad Max made it her personal crusade to find the boy before his powerful enemies did. The last thing she needed was journalist Davis Wolfe to meddle—but was this sexy cynic the key to saving the child's life?

SBCNM0306